Books by Vonna Harper

Carnal Secrets

Naked Nights
Her Submission
Taking Her Down

Taking Her Down

ISBN # 978-1-78686-129-0

©Copyright Vonna Harper 2017

Cover Art by Posh Gosh ©Copyright 2017

Interior text design by Claire Siemaszkiewicz

Totally Bound Publishing

This is a work of fiction. All characters, places and events are from the author's imagination and should not be confused with fact. Any resemblance to persons, living or dead, events or places is purely coincidental.

All rights reserved. No part of this publication may be reproduced in any material form, whether by printing, photocopying, scanning or otherwise without the written permission of the publisher, Totally Bound Publishing.

Applications should be addressed in the first instance, in writing, to Totally Bound Publishing. Unauthorised or restricted acts in relation to this publication may result in civil proceedings and/or criminal prosecution.

The author and illustrator have asserted their respective rights under the Copyright Designs and Patents Acts 1988 (as amended) to be identified as the author of this book and illustrator of the artwork.

Published in 2017 by Totally Bound Publishing, Newland House, The Point, Weaver Road, Lincoln, LN6 3QN, United Kingdom.

No part of this book may be reproduced, scanned, or distributed in any printed or electronic form without permission. Please do not participate in or encourage piracy of copyrighted materials in violation of the authors' rights. Purchase only authorised copies.

Totally Bound Publishing is a subsidiary of Totally Entwined Group Limited.

If you purchased this book without a cover you should be aware that this book is stolen property. It was reported as "unsold and destroyed" to the publisher and neither the author nor the publisher has received any payment for this "stripped book".

Carnal Secrets

TAKING HER DOWN

VONNA HARPER

Dedication

Loving thanks to my mother for gifting me with imagination, my sister for a lifetime of support, and the many writers who are part of this crazy journey.

Chapter One

Someone had tied the woman's wrists to either end of a long stick, effectively keeping her arms wide apart. She was naked, with large silicone breasts and a lean, almost skinny body. Sweat sealed her shoulder-length ash-blonde hair to her temples, and her eyes were nearly closed. Her head drooped.

At first, Shana thought the woman was out of it. Then the camera panned down her body to reveal her splayed legs and the moisture glistening on her sex. Her pussy was clean-shaven, the blatantly displayed flesh there darker than the rest of her — swollen from increased blood flow. The woman swayed. A long, low, satisfied moan rolled out of her.

"Shit," Shana whispered. "Shit."

"Wait," her friend Joleen said. "That's just the start."

Feeling flushed, Shana tightened her hold on her wine glass, brought it to her lips and gulped.

Several moments passed during which the woman on the monitor in Joleen's home office continued to sway and groan. Then she started to close her legs.

"No," a male voice commanded. "Keep them the way they are. I'm not done with you, not by a long shot."

The woman's eyes opened and she stared to her left, toward where Shana concluded the order had come from.

"I'm so tired." The woman licked her lips. "You're asking too much of me."

"Am I?" the unseen man shot back. "Maybe you'd like to be returned to the boat and from there to your vanilla life."

The woman lifted her restrained arms, only to let them

drop again. "No. Not yet."

"Not yet, what?"

Long, thick lashes fluttered. "No, I don't want to leave, Master."

"Shit. Seriously?"

Joleen shrugged. "You tell me. One thing I'm sure of, this isn't a porno flick with actors."

No, it wasn't. When Joleen had called, insisting she come over after work, her best friend had said little, except to explain that she'd used her considerable computer- hacking skills to find the password for a site Shana absolutely had to see. Joleen had even offered to supply the wine required for ultimate enjoyment. So, instead of formalizing a bid on a new landscaping project after her crew had left for the day, Shana had climbed into her pickup and headed for Joleen's place.

At a loss for words, Shana took another swallow and leaned closer to the screen. Not long ago she'd been worn out from a day that had started before dawn, but now she felt alive, anticipating something she couldn't wrap her mind around.

A tall, well-built and unselfconsciously naked man had just stepped into view. Shana expected his captive to shrink away when he extended a large hand toward her. Instead, she straightened and stood her ground. *Good for you,* Shana silently exhorted her. *Show him what you're made of.*

The man closed his right hand around the woman's throat and drew her to him, angling her head upward as he did. Their faces came closer. An impressive erect penis jabbed at the woman's belly.

A wave of heat, not entirely attributable to her wine, flowed into Shana as whoever these people were locked in a toe-curling kiss. Granted, the woman didn't have much choice in the matter but, unless Shana couldn't read body language, she was enjoying herself. A lot.

Roll with it, lady. Rock the experience.

Lips crushed lips. Two mouths separated. The bound

woman rose onto her toes, making no attempt to free herself from the fingers on her neck. Inch by inch, the larger player, if that's what they were, forced her to lean back until she was off balance. Her shoulders strained from the effort of trying to lift her arms, but the invading masculine body made that impossible.

At the last moment, he saved her from falling by letting go and grabbing the stick. He deftly drew her arms over her head and secured the stick to a hook dangling from a rope Shana hadn't noticed.

"What have you done?" The woman struggled to free herself, which caused her expensive breasts to jiggle. Her barely there belly sucked in and out.

"Keeping you handy." The man stepped to her side, took hold of her hair and pulled down on it until she was staring upward. "You impressed me with your efforts to remain in place while I played with you." His free hand slipped between her legs. "But now that I have you, my options have increased."

Anchored and helpless to stop the man from doing anything and everything he wanted to. *What the hell would that feel like?*

Is that something I'd ever want to experience?

Joleen clicked the mouse to freeze the action. The nameless couple remained locked in anticipation, with the man's body so close Shana longed to touch him. He wasn't particularly handsome, with thick, graying hair that covered his chest and belly. He had a bit of a paunch and appeared to be in his late forties, with muscled arms and thighs that said he lived a physical life.

As the owner of her own landscaping company, Shana spent her days around more men than women. Ordinarily, this one wouldn't have warranted a second look, but then those who worked for her came fully dressed.

More to the point, in her day job she was the boss, while this member of the male sex was definitely in charge.

Another hot wave ran through her.

"I've done some research." Joleen sounded out of breath. "This isn't one of those membership porn sites and those two aren't being paid for their *efforts*."

"Then what are they?"

"Near as I can tell, this site hasn't been given a formal name. The URL contains the letters MSDB, which could be BDSM reversed. That particular activity has gotten so much play lately that I can't imagine them being concerned the morality patrol might shut them down." She paused. "Just the same, I can't help wondering if whatever MSDB is about goes beyond submission and Dominance."

Shana struggled to concentrate on what she'd just been told—no easy task, considering the electrical charges striking her from all directions. Damn, what practices existed in a culture she'd never dreamed of—well, hardly ever.

"What do you mean by 'beyond'?" she belatedly thought to ask.

Joleen winked. "Okay, truth is, instead of working this afternoon, I watched several other, ah, scenes. Wow to the max. Boy, have I been living a sheltered life."

"Sheltered from what?"

Joleen shook her head. "Oh no you don't. I'm not going to give anything away. You have to watch some of those scenes if you want to know what I'm talking about, except 'scenes' probably isn't the right term."

Talking had helped separate Shana a little from the crazy thought that she *had* to explore what MSDB was about. "So, speaking hypothetically, where would one go for more information?"

Joleen lightly punched her arm. "Hypothetically, my ass. For starters, they frequently mention an island."

Guessing Joleen knew more than she was letting on, Shana decided to play along. "The man said something about a boat."

"Yeah. Parts of the scenes—I watched four of them in between taking breaks to work off a little steam—were filmed out of doors. No one seemed to be cold and the vegetation is tropical."

"And the site is located where? Come on, you know how to find out that kind of thing."

"Indeed I do." Joleen patted herself on the shoulder. "Florida."

Shana blinked. "Seriously?"

"Hey, I wouldn't joke about that."

She and Joleen lived on Florida's east coast. Quite possibly, the videos had been shot not far from there, maybe on one of the numerous nearby islands.

"I'm assuming everything that takes place is consensual," Joleen said. "At least I hope to hell it is."

Bondage? Maybe the real thing? The thought made her shiver. "What makes you say that?"

"Because some of what happens is damn intense."

She could have asked what constituted 'intense' but she preferred to determine that on her own, in private.

Joleen minimized the frozen naked couple and opened another screen. This one consisted of a paragraph of text.

The majority of women have secret sexual cravings. Unfortunately, most live their entire lives never giving those cravings free rein. Fear, inertia, and lack of opportunity hold them back. As a result they don't know what it means to be truly alive. To take great risks.

If you have courage, strength and need – welcome.

"How do you read that?" Joleen asked. "Are they looking for new clients or customers or – or maybe, I don't know, something?"

Shana stopped looking at the monitor so she could give her friend her full attention. A self-professed geek, Joleen ran her own Internet security business. Her clients paid her to assume all responsibility for keeping their firewalls up to date. She thrived on staying ahead of hackers. Ignorant and demanding clients drove her crazy but, because she had student loans to repay, she kept her mouth shut and dreamed of the day when she could pick and choose who she worked with.

Shana, too, dreamed of being able to work only on projects that fed her creativity, unlike the one she'd just completed for the county airport. Seriously, junipers and more junipers!

"Wait a minute," she said. "You can't be thinking of getting in touch with whoever these people are."

Joleen smiled. "Have more wine and watch a little longer. Then we'll see if you're still asking the same question."

When her friend maximized the screen, Shana shoved Joleen's comment to the back of her mind and focused on the resumed action. She also kept after her wine.

The man released some of the tension on the woman's hair, but not enough that she could stand upright. The captive tried twisting in one direction, then the other, not that it did her any good because of her restraints. Her size D breasts were spectacular, she had artificial nails, and her toenails were painted a glistening silver. Even with her hair trapped in the man's paw, Shana could see the highlights and expensive cut.

So, this woman with rope around her wrists, her head wrenched back and a man's hand hard against her pussy was used to spending money on herself. If only her friends could see her now.

"You're spoiled," the man told her. "Used to getting everything your way."

"Yes, Master."

Struck by the submissive tone with undercurrents of sexual excitement, Shana stopped studying the kind of breasts she'd never in a million years be able to afford and turned her attention to the woman's expression. She didn't act scared. Hell, she didn't even appear to be nervous.

Barely aware of what she was doing, Shana closed the fingers of her right hand around her left wrist. What would restraints feel like?

What would they do to her sense of self?

Her libido?

"Those days of pampering yourself are behind you, slave," the man continued. "From now on, I call all the shots. You're mine to play with, to punish when and how I want. To get rid of if you bore me. Do you understand?"

"Yes, Master."

He chuckled. "You think I'm playing into your hands, but you're wrong. I'm not your sugar daddy. I'm your Master."

The woman's eyes closed again and her mouth sagged open. Unless Shana was mistaken, she was in subspace. Anticipating. Waiting. Wanting.

She wasn't the only one.

When the woman's nostrils flared, Shana concentrated on what else the man was doing. His hand between her legs was on the move, sliding back and forth, back and forth, going faster and faster.

Imagining the same thing happening to her just about drove her crazy. Her panties' cotton crotch lay over her sex, held tightly in place by the jeans she wore seven days a week. She didn't much care whether Joleen was aware of what she was doing as she rocked toward and away from the desk to increase the friction on her labia. She tightened muscles that hadn't held a man for longer than she wanted to think about.

"He doesn't do anything for me." Joleen's voice sounded rough. "If I ever signed up for a service, or whatever the hell they call it, I'd insist on someone with less back hair. A bigger cock wouldn't be bad either."

Shana mentally switched places with the naked woman. She felt the strain in her arms and dirt and grass under her feet. Most of all, she felt what the man was doing, the rub of male fingers against hot female flesh.

Suddenly, she didn't care what 'Master' looked like, whether he spoke or never said another word. What mattered was that he stood beside her. Touched her.

Controlled her.

The mysterious man she was conjuring up understood the female body far better than she did. He knew when to slip a finger into her drenched opening and when to paint her with her own juices. His breath on the side of her neck made her break out in goosebumps and instinctively fight the unrelenting restraints. 'Master' had no doubt of her desperate need to climax and how to keep her trembling on the brink. Denying her the one thing she needed in life. Glaring, the domineering man ignored her pleas, and when she cursed him, he slapped her breasts.

Kept her.

Kept? Where did that come from?

"So." Joleen made the word last a long time. "I take it you're glad I called."

Her gaze resolutely on the monitor where the woman twitched and danced on the finger rammed deep inside her, Shana poured herself another glass. "Shit, yes."

Her friend filled her own glass without taking her attention off the action. "We're sick."

"Not sick. Horny." *And more.*

Joleen sighed and started stroking her throat. "Unfortunately, the condition goes with the territory. Neither of us has the time to pick up a man, let alone do whatever it takes to get and hold a boyfriend."

Cursing the denim in the way, Shana ran her fingers over her lower belly. "Give me the URL for the site and the password. I know how I'm going to be spending the night."

"Understandable." Joleen studied what Shana was doing. "But I have to warn you, they undoubtedly monitor traffic. They'll figure out who you are. Maybe they can learn all kinds of things about you."

"Just like they have about you?"

Joleen laughed. "Is that a serious question?"

No, she decided, it wasn't. If anyone knew how to keep their identity secret online, it was Joleen.

"I don't give a damn what happens," she admitted. "My voyeuristic activities aren't against the law, are they?"

"Not as far as I know."

They could have debated the issue, but she didn't care and, she suspected, neither did her friend. Her sexual experiences, starting with when she'd lost her virginity the night of her senior prom, hadn't prepared her for what she was seeing. Granted, she hadn't been living under a rock and had read most of *Fifty Shades of Grey*, but this was new.

Challenging her to go where she'd never gone before.

"What do you think?" she asked, because if she didn't say something she didn't trust herself to keep her jeans zipped. "If you couldn't hide behind anonymity, would you check things out?"

Joleen frowned. "It depends on what you mean by 'checking things out'. People can subscribe to the videos if they pass the application process. There's also an interactive component."

There was? Her throat dried at the thought of getting in contact with the organization, or whatever it was. At the same time, watching Ms. Boobs and Hairy Back wasn't enough. Putting off responding, she let her fingers slide a little lower while concentrating on the action. Hairy Back had moved to the woman's left breast. After licking his fingers, he lightly rolled her nipple between thumb and forefinger, keeping his attention riveted on her face. The man continued his assault on her sex.

Shana understood control. She'd spent the past five years building her company one private yard or small business at a time. She succeeded, not just because she knew a great deal about what thrived in humid climates, but because she had a business head. She selected and kept employees with strong work ethics. Equally important, she listened to prospective clients and knew what questions to ask to draw out their preferences. No part of the business escaped her attention. No detail was too small. She answered to a multitude of masters, but at the end of the day, she was her own harshest critic.

Master.

Turning her body over to someone else, a male someone.

Tapping into her sexuality in ways she'd barely dared imagine.

"What are you thinking?" Joleen asked. "Any chance you're trying to imagine what it would feel like to be in the woman's position?"

Pulled back into the here and now, Shana blinked and again focused on the action. Hairy Back leaned down and closed his lips around his captive's right breast, while continuing to grip the other one. His hand remained against her sex. The woman shuddered and her head fell back. A moment later, she straightened, then backed away as far as she could, followed by sagging in her bonds.

"Oh God, oh God," she moaned. "Please, please…"

"Think he's biting her?" Shana asked.

"Is she acting like she's being hurt?"

Hardly. In fact, if sounds and action were any indication, Ms. Boobs was having the ride of her life. She rocked her hips in a blatant invitation to be taken deeper. She repeatedly closed and opened her legs while bobbing her head in rhythm with the finger fucking. She said "Please" about a million times. Every time she did, Hairy Back redoubled his attack.

"Holy shit," Joleen hissed. "This is even better the second time."

Eyes glued to the action, Shana wondered if she had what it took to get through the video once, let alone repeatedly. And Joleen had said there were a number of videos.

Ms. Boobs let out a scream that hurt Shana's ears. The captive's body shook and shivered. A thin line of drool dribbled from the sides of her mouth. Feeling Ms. Boobs' climax throughout her own body, Shana pushed her middle finger as hard as she could against her slit. *Double damn my clothes!*

"So — whew, so do you think she got off?" Joleen asked.

Shana snorted. "Ah, duh. Yeah, I'd say she did."

"That's the conclusion I came to. Damn, I need to get laid."

Joleen's cheeks were flushed and she seemed to be having trouble keeping her eyes open. Shana was torn between watching the rest of the action here and being alone.

Alone with her sex toys. Facing a part of her she only rarely acknowledged.

When Joleen, again, stopped the action, it took considerable effort on Shana's part not to demand she hit Play. The slightly blurred images on the monitor had a disembodied quality, as if the couple — was that what she should call them? — might never finish what they'd started.

It sure as hell wouldn't be like that if she were part of the action.

If she accepted the challenge.

"More wine?" Joleen asked. "We could order pizza and — I was going to say we could have our own orgy but that's a kink I can't imagine being involved in with you."

"I feel the same way." Joleen was the sister she hadn't had, not someone she wanted to have a homosexual experience with. She groaned. "Unfortunately, I have to get up at five."

"Hmm." Joleen pointedly stared at Shana's still-on-her-crotch hand. "You sure you're thinking about work?"

Shana gave her slit another stroke then reluctantly stood. "Maybe not."

Joleen grabbed a sticky note and started writing on it. "No maybe to it, girlfriend. It'll be interesting to see if either of us gets any sleep tonight. I'm giving you the URL and password for MSDB. If you decide to do more than watch, let me know. Safety and all that."

Snagged by Joleen's warning tone, Shana tucked the small yellow square into her pocket. "I will. The same goes for you."

Chuckling, Joleen lightly punched her arm. "Why do you think I let you in on this, whatever it is?"

"You're serious? You're going to give MSDB a try?"

"I don't know. What about you?"

As Shana slid her hands into her back pockets, her gaze returned to the interrupted action. There was no mistaking

Ms. Boobs' mood. The woman with her arms forced over her head was having the time of her life. Maybe experiencing the most intense orgasm she'd ever had.

"Let me watch some more action," Shana belatedly answered. "Then I'll let you know."

"You really think you could handle giving up control?"

"Being the boss isn't always what it's cracked up to be."

"True, but that isn't what we're talking about. This is my body." She gripped her arms. "Even with the obvious benefits"—she jerked her head at the monitor—"I can't imagine becoming a man's slave."

Slave. Sex slave? More object than woman? Forced to be primitive.

Challenged.

She wrapped strong fingers around her wrist.

Caught.

Changed.

Chapter Two

"Done and done."

Ward glanced up from the brief he'd been trying to concentrate on. Jim, his partner in their legal firm, stood in the doorway.

"The judge signed off on the verdict?" he asked. Glad for the interruption, he stood, stretched and walked over to the window with its less-than-spectacular view of the parking lot.

Jim joined him. "The last 'T' has been crossed. You and I are going to celebrate."

Celebrating usually meant walking over to Guilty, the upscale bar a few blocks from where most of the city's legal offices were clustered. Most times Ward limited himself to going there only on Friday nights, but ever since taking on the case against a construction company that had broken their contract to handle a major paving project, he'd been putting in fifty-hour weeks.

"I'm serious," Jim pressed. "I'm of a mind to tie one on and I wasn't the lead on the damn complicated case. Drink yourself stupid and call a cab."

He was tempted, but not just because a celebration was in order. Truth was, he couldn't remember ever feeling this burned out. In fact, he was questioning his career, asking whether there was more to life than going to bat for the firm's clients. Whiskey would undoubtedly blunt the edges of those questions. Maybe by Monday he'd, again, give a damn.

"I might," he muttered. It had been spring when the fraud allegations had hit his desk. Now, if the falling leaves were any indication, it was fall. A whole summer lost.

A life on hold.

Jim's hand landed on his shoulder, prompting him to turn toward the man who was as much friend as partner. At six foot three inches, Ward was taller than most men, including Jim, who insisted he was six foot when he was at least two inches shorter than that.

"I'm worried about you," Jim said.

"Yeah?"

"Yeah. There was a spark missing even before this case blew up. I thought diving into it might do the trick but, in some respects, you phoned in your work. That isn't like you."

If anyone else had said that he might have punched him, but he and Jim had few secrets. Like it or not, his fellow lawyer was right.

He shrugged. "Midlife crises."

"At thirty-six, I don't think so. Damn it, she wasn't worth it."

"I'm over her," he said of the female detective he'd had a vanilla relationship with for over a year. "No torches being carried."

"And you're the wiser for the experience. At least, I hope you are."

"I am. What I need is a vacation. Maybe get in some fishing before winter."

Jim rolled his eyes. "There's fishing and then there's fishing. Why don't you hook into something worth the effort? How long has it been since you offered your services at MSDB?"

Two years.

For reasons no one knew about.

Reasons that, even today, sent equal waves of tension and anticipation through him.

"Maybe I will," he said around a dark need stronger than anything he'd ever felt for his career.

"Don't 'maybe' me. You want my opinion and, even if

you don't, some time on the island spent doing what you excel at is exactly what you need and want."

His friend was the one person in his social circle who knew what he'd been doing before Melissa had entered his life. When things had started getting serious between them, he'd known he needed to sever his relationship with MSDB. Being loyal to Melissa had turned him into someone he barely knew and had little control over.

On the rare occasions when he didn't want to own up to responsibility for his dark side, he gave a shot at blaming Jim. After all, Jim had gotten him in the front door – not that there were many doors on the island – after a liquor-fueled weekend that had included overdosing on porn flicks. Thinking back on those forty-eight hours, Ward knew Jim had been testing him. Once Jim had realized he had a more than casual interest in Domination and Dominating, Jim had come clean about his own involvement with the lifestyle.

Jim did more than fantasize about controlling a submissive woman like Ward had been doing. Jim was part of the BDSM scene and, as such, was willing and able to start Ward down the same road.

"I've been thinking about going back in," Ward admitted. "Of course, I haven't had time for anything except the case from Hell for months."

"But now?"

But now he did, *if* he could handle, let alone control, that side of him. "Don't push me."

"Me, push? Never. Okay, yes, when I know I'm right."

Did Jim? Would he say the same thing if he knew Ward compared his fascination with Domination to a drug addiction?

"What is it?" he shot back. "You get a bonus for getting me to sign up for another round?"

"I wish. They've been asking about you, saying you're a natural."

"Have they?" Despite his need to concentrate on the

conversation and his reaction to it, his mind took its own journey to the private island with a half-dozen cabins nestled in jungle-like growth and a larger building that, from the outside, appeared to be a restaurant. The only access to the island was by boat and there was only a single dock with a well-paid guard who made sure anyone who didn't belong didn't step ashore.

Or leave, if that wasn't part of the plan.

"Yes, they have," Jim said. "You know you want to tie up whatever *client* catches your attention and take a whip to her. A few hours of that, highlighted by filling her holes, and you'll be back to the old you. Plus, you won't have to clean the damn fish."

He chuckled. The past year had been the most intense of his life, emotionally and intellectually exhausting. Between admitting he wasn't built for ordinary man-woman relationships and pulling together the complex case, he'd been lucky to remember to brush his teeth. Returning to a single status had taken place several months ago, but he hadn't had time to process what that truly meant. Now, as of this morning's verdict, a major professional weight was off his shoulders.

The beast inside might awaken.

Hell, it already had.

And was calling to him.

"Look at it this way," Jim pressed. "A little Dom action's a hell of a lot more satisfying than going to a shrink. Admit it, you need to get laid."

There was no denying that.

"That isn't all. Imagine a woman's mouth around your pecker and your cuffs on her wrists. What more do you want in life?"

Maybe nothing.

Maybe this time being called 'Master' would be enough.

"What's the hesitation?" Jim demanded.

Turning his back to the window, Ward faced the other man. "Answer me something, all right? No brushing off what I'm going to say."

Jim's features sobered. "All right. What is it?"

He clenched his fingers and filled his lungs. "Do you ever get the feeling there's something about the island?" He worked up a casual shrug, but the gesture did nothing to release his tension. "Maybe it's knowing there wouldn't be anything left of it if a hurricane hit."

"That's true."

"Maybe that's why I don't get the best vibes about the place."

Jim held his gaze for a moment before staring at the ground. "Funny you should mention that. I sometimes feel trapped there. No wonder I do. We're at the mercy of whoever is running the boats. If something happened, we couldn't get off."

True, but that wasn't the only reason being on the mainland was easier on his nervous system. The island wasn't tiny, but he could probably walk around it in a day. Was it possible to feel claustrophobic when surrounded by miles and miles of ocean?

"That's it?" he asked. "You worry about an escape route or lack of one?"

Jim nodded. "Do you blame me?"

"Hell, no. I did some research on the island. Apparently, Native Americans never lived there? Considering there's a natural bowl perfect for capturing rain water, plus all the birds and reptiles, don't you think some tribe would have claimed it? Their enemies couldn't sneak up on them."

"Are you saying the Natives knew — what are you saying, that spirits or something scared them off?"

'Spirits'. He wouldn't go that far. What he did know was he'd avoided the island because he didn't feel in charge there.

As if something was trying to take control of his mind and let the beast out.

Chapter Three

Shana wiped sweaty hands on her jeans and stared at the rapidly approaching island. The dock didn't appear large enough to handle the pleasure boat she was on. Ever since learning that her application had been approved, she'd repeatedly told herself this was what she wanted. She'd expected nerves. She just hadn't realized they'd be this intense.

Taking her attention off the tropical vegetation growing within a few feet of the shore, she glanced at the other two women who'd be sharing this adventure with her. They'd said little of a personal nature during the hour-long trip. What she did know was that both women were professionals eager for what one of them had called 'a hell of an adventure and enough sex to last a year'.

Iva, if that was her real name, had been the more vocal of the two, but now she was as quiet as Genice. Both were what Shana considered high-maintenance women. She hadn't been surprised when they'd talked more to each other than they had to her. That was fine, since long ago she'd realized she had little in common with women who knew, let alone cared, what clothes were in fashion.

What the hell am I doing here? Not only did the growth appear impenetrable, but she hadn't fully grasped the guidelines she'd been sent after she'd arranged for a bank transfer to pay for her adventure. She understood why she'd had to submit a medical report showing she was in good physical and mental health, as well as free of sexual diseases. She hoped the statement about the man she'd been paired with was true. According to the guidelines, she could pull the plug on the operation whenever she wanted by calling out the word 'red'. It would be picked up by a listening device. Otherwise, the exercises — that's what they called them — would increase in intensity until maximum stress and pleasure was achieved.

'Maximum stress and pleasure'? What kind of word salad nonsense is that?

"Crap." Genice settled herself next to Shana and gripped the railing. "I didn't think I'd be this nervous."

"Me either," Iva said from Genice's other side. "My cousin said it would be the ride of my life but she refused to elaborate. And when I asked if she'd join me, she said 'hell no'. We never were that close. If she…"

"You aren't saying she might have sold you out, are you?" Genice asked.

"No." Iva didn't sound sure. "No, she wouldn't."

The videos Joleen had introduced her to had been hot to the max, so hot she'd watched them every night for a week, while treating herself to multiple orgasms. Then, she'd scored two new landscaping contracts and been so busy there'd been no time for self-satisfaction. Now, those projects were winding down and she'd pretty much cleared her agenda for twenty-four hours, give or take a few. It wasn't much, but the way she saw it, twenty-four hours of not having to think about work constituted a vacation.

After talking herself in and out of trying to see what MSDB was about more times than she wanted to admit, she'd filled in the online application. That had been the start of some whirlwind activity, including more soul-searching and reminders that she'd never backed down from a challenge and shouldn't start now.

Here she was. Bracing herself as the craft bumped the dock. Smelling a wealth of plants, trees and swampy earth. Straining to make out the path that had to lead to the cottage where she'd be staying.

Not just staying.

Learning why the thought of wearing cuffs and rope

turned her on.

"I wonder if we'll see each other," Iva said.

Genice took a less-than-steady breath. "There's that community room where food's kept and where everyone has to check in from time to time. Maybe we'll bump into each other."

As the boat motor cut out, Shana impulsively grabbed both women's hands and squeezed. They returned the gesture. She might have said something if a tall, slender man, wearing tan shorts and a collared shirt, wasn't tying their craft to the dock. He seemed overdressed for the task. Unlike the captain, who'd barely acknowledged them, this man looked more approachable.

Unfortunately, she wasn't sure she could trust her instincts on that.

The slim man picked up a ramp and hooked it over the side of the boat. He beckoned the women to join him.

"Are we ready for this, ladies?" Genice asked.

Iva took a backward step. "I guess. I wish they would have sent me a picture of the hunk I'll be working with. I asked and asked. All I got for my trouble was a one word answer. I'm sure you know what it was."

Shana hadn't asked for a picture, but she'd nearly backed out when she'd been informed that MSDB wasn't in the business of supplying background information about their male operatives. 'Operatives'? What the hell did that mean? She could understand a Dominant. At least she was comfortable with the concept.

Irritated at herself for stalling, she fell in line behind the other two women.

"Welcome, ladies," their host said, once they were on the dock. "It's eighty-two degrees today with a humidity of not quite forty percent which, considering the time of year, is quite pleasant. Everything has been made ready for you. Your education is about to begin."

"'Education'?" Genice asked. "I thought the word was adventure."

He shrugged and smiled. "I dare say by the time your opportunity to return to the mainline comes you'll admit it has been both. Now" — he studied each of them in turn — "for the record, I need to hear you say you're here of your own free will and have no doubt that your wellbeing is our priority. No matter what happens — well, I won't elaborate on that, because anticipation is half of the fun. No reservations?"

Shana started to nod but, damn it, being in unfamiliar territory was no reason to wimp out. "No reservations," she said.

He smiled. "Shana, right?"

"How did you know?" she asked.

Long fingers circled her wrist. "Those are the hands of a woman who earns her living with them."

The man's hand felt nothing like hers had when she'd done the same thing. She nearly jerked free of the intimate contact, but he was undoubtedly judging her reaction. No way would she fail this first test.

She was here to learn the meaning of the word 'submissive'.

Maybe understand herself better.

Head cocked, the man regarded her while slowly tightening his grip. Iva's sharp intake of breath told her the other woman was aware of what was happening. No way did she want her blood flow cut off but, until or unless that happened, she'd experience. Besides, she could probably break free and, hopefully, her fellow travelers would come to her aid. Those things helped settle her. More to the point, she was getting her first taste of what MSDB Island was about.

Exciting.

Unnerving.

"Good," the man said and released her. "Now, for a few housekeeping items. There's a separate path leading from here to each cabin and those paths go through some of the island's densest vegetation. Tropical growth serves as a natural buffer between every cabin so you'll be assured of complete privacy."

And no one knowing what the others are experiencing.

Whether they're all right.

"What about the main building?" Ivy's voice sounded higher than it had earlier.

"Your Dominant will take you to it for certain activities, but most of your training will take place in isolated and secure settings."

By 'secure', did he mean they were assured of privacy or because they couldn't escape? She'd weathered moments of doubt before, about this so-called adventure, but they'd reared their heads when she'd been at home. Now she was on alien turf, on an island controlled by forces she didn't comprehend.

What the hell am I doing here?

Chapter Four

Shana could no longer see Genice or Iva. At the man's direction, they'd each started down a separate path. Within seconds, the wilderness had swallowed them. Her heart pounding, Shana split her attention between trying to avoid the vines encroaching on the crushed seashell trail and straining to see what was around the next curve. The tropical smell was overpowering. Massive cypress trees and wild pines hid the sky. Being well-versed in natural vegetation, she knew it took frequent trimming to keep the thin walkway from being overtaken. She couldn't help but imagine trying to escape, only to find herself trapped by the wilderness.

Who was waiting for her at the cabin that had been selected for her? Would it be the designated Dominant? Hopefully, there'd be a housekeeper, maybe a worldly but easy-going older woman willing to fill in the considerable blanks in what little she knew about what she'd gotten herself into.

Damn it, she should have done more research. Given herself time to reflect on what MSDB was about before committing.

But she hadn't, because she'd sensed she would have talked herself out of the adventure, or education, or whatever this was, and would spend the rest of her life wondering what she'd missed.

Continue taking responsibility for her business and life when a part of her needed someone else to assume that role.

Someone who understood her needs more intimately than she did.

"Shana."

Startled, she stopped and stared in the direction she thought the voice had come from. Her cheeks flushed, which was understandable. She couldn't say the same for her suddenly hard nipples.

"What? Who is it? Where are you?"

When no one answered, she wondered if she'd imagined she'd heard her name being spoken. After all, a million insects, to say nothing of untold birds, sang a loud and never-ending song. She needed to start walking again but didn't.

Damn it, why had she agreed to so much uncertainty?

Because she needed to surrender control.

She filled her lungs with heavy, damp air. "Is someone there?"

"Why are you here?"

Something about the deep, low and primitive-sounding masculine voice snapped her nerve endings to attention and tightened her nipples even more.

"I might ask you the same question," she finally came up with.

"You could, but I'm not going to answer. You are. What brought you to the island?"

Don't back down! Give as good as you get for as long as you can. "I like a challenge."

"Not enough." He sounded angry. "How did you learn about MSDB?"

She told him, but didn't name Joleen. "I submitted my application and it was approved. I'm sure you know that."

"I assumed. For your information, I know almost nothing about you. How tall are you, five foot seven?"

Undoubtedly, this was his way of telling her he was studying her. Fighting the urge to wrap her arms around her waist in a self-protective gesture, she nodded. "Close enough. How tall are you?"

"I ask the questions. Back to my question about why you're here. Viewing some of our videos triggered something inside you. Describe that something."

The contract she'd signed had included a paragraph about how being honest both with herself and the person in charge of her 'education' would maximize her experience. Back then, she'd wondered why whoever had developed the contract hadn't been more specific. She still didn't have an answer.

"I don't know if I can." Insects buzzed around her, prompting her to wave her hands to keep them from landing. "I'm goal-oriented. I have my own business with plans to expand it. That hasn't left much time for a personal life."

"Personal life? Your sexual one, you mean."

She nodded.

"What do you want out of your time here?"

She hadn't expected this. On the brink of saying she wasn't sure, she took a moment to dig deeper.

"I need a greater understanding of myself. I said I'm goal-oriented but sometimes, when I think about living my entire life running or trying to run the show, it feels daunting." She dug her sandal into the tiny pieces of seashell. "I've even joked I wouldn't mind being a kept woman."

"All that money for spreading your legs?"

"No," she insisted. "My sugar daddy doesn't have to be rich. I just want—damn, this isn't easy to say, but a part of me wants to put that non-existent man's needs before my own. Pleasing him might complete me." *Did I really say that?* "At least I'd like to have a chance to find out if it's true."

"What about turning your body over to him?"

Sweat trickled down her back. Between the bugs and heat she was having trouble concentrating—either that, or he'd asked something she wasn't ready to face after all.

"I guess that's for you to offer and for me to experience."

"It isn't that simple."

Swallowing took effort. "No, I don't suppose it is."

"All right. I know everything I need to for now. Get moving."

How could he say what he had? She hadn't told him

anything important, had she?

Wishing she didn't feel so conflicted, she started walking again. Knowing she was being watched was unnerving. At the same time, her awareness of herself as a sexual creature kicked up a notch. She wasn't a knockout, but she wasn't bad-looking either, and she was in decent physical shape. Before long she'd be naked and he'd—

How would she go from dressed to nude? Maybe he'd order her to strip. Maybe he'd do the disrobing while she stood before him, shivering like a virgin. Would he immediately get rid of his own clothes or remain clothed as a statement about the difference in their status?

Was it too late to change her mind?

Even before she spotted the structure set up on stilts, she'd answered her question. She was nervous, that was all. Anyone who didn't know what to expect in this situation would be.

No way would she back down.

She climbed the half dozen steps then gripped the porch railing and turned around. No matter how intently she studied her surroundings, she saw no sign of another human being. The prickling down her spine left no doubt that unseen eyes were on her.

The man was stalking her.

He'd hunted her down and now she was where he wanted her.

The unsettling thought stripped her of too much strength. Telling herself that her imagination was responsible didn't begin to relax her. She'd have been a fool to discount anything instinct was trying to tell her.

Time to see what was beyond the cabin door.

She filled her lungs, turned her back to the wilderness and closed her numb hand around the knob. It turned. The door swung inward. Holding her breath, she tightened her grip and slowly entered.

Large, open but screened windows took up most of the space on all four walls. An overhead fan stirred the humid air. The room wasn't much bigger than her bedroom, with a minimum of furniture—two large, well-made chairs and an oversized couch. A hand-carved wooden storage chest painted in shades of red and black served as a coffee table. There was nothing on the table, no paintings on the walls. The stark quality said this wasn't a place for living.

Neither was it set up for sex play.

Memories of the MSDB videos flooded her until she had no doubt what she'd find behind the closed door on the far side of the room. The bedroom was in there—more than a bedroom, she amended, a place for every erotic activity she could think of and more.

No way was she going to check it out yet.

Keeping her back to the hidden room, she started to close the front door behind her. It pressed against her. Startled, she scrambled away. Hand to her throat, she whirled to face whoever had been on the outside.

The tall, tan man filling the doorway wore black shorts and a white collared shirt. He had sandals on. A length of rope dangled from strong fingers.

Rope meant for her.

A gasp threatened to break free. She fought to keep it buried. Her hands became fists, nails digging into her palms. He fixed a harsh, gray-eyed glare on her.

"Don't." He indicated her fists. "I'm in charge, not you."

Wasn't there supposed to be some kind of introduction, a discussion about the ground rules, a few quiet minutes before the storm?

The man wasn't huge, but she concluded he outweighed her by close to a hundred pounds. Between his height and the width of his shoulders, she didn't stand a chance against him. His dark brown hair had recently been professionally cut, his hands showed no sign of physical labor and his clothing was expensive. The thought might have been crazy, yet she couldn't help but wonder if he were a lawyer.

A lawyer with a need to control?

"Get a good look, did you?" he demanded. "For the

record, I have all my own teeth and my eyesight is twenty-twenty."

Maybe he'd intended the comment as a joke, but until she knew him better — if that was going to happen — she'd simply watch and learn.

"What do you think?" He indicated the room.

"I — There isn't much to it."

"That's because the effort went into the bedroom. You'll see it soon enough."

She would when he'd decided it was time. How much more was he determined to be in charge of?

Chapter Five

"Good." He drew out the word. "Submissives who ask a lot of questions piss me off. Listen and learn. Experience and assess. That's the only thing you have to do."

She wondered if his comment and presentation were designed to keep emotional distance between them. If so, that was fine with her, since she had no intention of checking him out on Facebook. Besides, how could she, when she didn't know his name, let alone what he did for a living or why he was involved with MSDB.

He took a slow step toward her. "First things first. Getting rid of your clothes."

Suddenly angry, she stood her ground. "What? No. That can't be the first thing."

The beginning of a cool smile lifted his lips, only to be replaced by something dark. "It's what I say it is. Either you strip or I do it for you."

Excitement lanced her. Damn it, yes, this was what she'd signed up for—even if it killed her.

"I read the rules," she countered. "You aren't supposed to do anything I disapprove of."

"Oh, you'll approve. And you'll keep everything that happens here to yourself."

She waited for another wave of excitement that would tell her the games had begun, but it didn't happen. On edge, she took in everything she could of the man standing between her and freedom. In sharp contrast to his professional vibes, there was something primal about him. A cave-like depth. When he was on the island, this man did what he wanted to. He had no concern for the consequences and no interest in her beyond getting her to submit to him.

"Why wouldn't I tell anyone?" she finally thought to ask.

"You'll understand, eventually."

This was crazy. Nothing was going like she'd told herself it would. Emotionally off balance, she curled her toes in an attempt to keep from bolting.

"All right," she said. "Show me."

His attention flicked to the window to his right. It had to be the lighting and her nerves, but for a moment she swore she was seeing a predator instead of a human. This creature would stalk and capture and control.

She was still trying to shake off the crazy thought when he charged. He grabbed her around the waist and pushed her back and off her feet. She landed on her ass on the couch.

"What the hell!" She reached for his neck but, before she could dig her fingers into his throat, if that had been her intention, he flipped her so she was sprawled the length of the couch on her belly and planted his knee against the base of her spine.

More disbelieving than terrified, she wrenched her head to the side so she could breathe. He was so close she saw only a blur. His weight bore down on her, making it impossible for her to do more than flex her knees. Her right arm was caught between her body and the couch back but, maybe, if she tried hard enough, she could grab his cock with her left and inflict—

Too-big fingers clamped around her left wrist and wrenched her arm behind her. Despite her give-it-all-she-had struggles, he captured her other wrist and brought it back as well.

"Pay attention." Moist breath dampened the back of her neck. "I strongly recommend you not forget anything about what I'm doing. It'll make what comes after easier to accept."

I'm not your damn play toy! Determined to regain use of her arms, she strained to free them.

"So you like to fight, do you? Fine with me. The thing is,

I always win."

Bucking and kicking, she put all her strength into trying to get him off her. The couch was so soft she felt as if she were sinking into it, which she might if he leaned more heavily against her. As her muscles started trembling, she'd come to the not too brilliant conclusion that he must be taunting her. He placed one of her wrists over the other so he could control both of them with a single hand. She debated trying to dig her nails into his thigh but he'd probably make her pay for it.

Pay for it. A captive's punishment.

Out of breath, she stopped fighting. She prayed he'd let up on the pressure. When he didn't, she slipped into the sensation. A part of her wondered if he might not be associated with MSDB but had snuck onto the island so he could play his sick game, but she didn't see how that was possible. Once this, whatever it was, had played itself out, he'd explain the rationale behind this rough and raw approach.

They'd move on to the next lesson.

"On a scale of one to ten," he said, "how scared are you?"

Good question. Designed to bring her back to Earth. "Maybe a four."

"Or higher. I'm going to add more elements. Then I'll determine whether your fear barometer goes up or down."

He released her wrists and leaned to the side, so he could pick something off the floor. She couldn't see what it was and didn't want to know. Then he looped rope around her arms just above her elbows and tightened the strands.

"Damn it, no!" She fought to pull her arms free.

"Yes." The rope pressed against her flesh, drawing her elbows close together. The strength that allowed her to work alongside her employees was useless because she couldn't get any leverage. Growing strain in her shoulders caught her attention and she forced herself to relax.

"I'm not going to dislocate anything." He patted her cheek. "Fortunately for you, I'm well trained in what the female body is capable of. Sometimes, I even take that into consideration."

"What are you talking about?"

"I intend to keep you under control, and this is the most efficient means of accomplishing my goal — for now."

He'd been doing something to the rope while he'd been talking. She tried to separate her arms. They went nowhere, refused to move. Two rope strands had been sealed against her flesh between her shoulders and elbows, rendering her upper limbs useless.

Why the hell hadn't she blurted out the safe word? If she'd yelled "Red", she'd have been out of this mess.

"This way," he said as he got off her, "you're less likely to injure yourself and I'm more likely to enjoy — yes, enjoy. Have to remember that."

A sigh of relief escaped her now that his weight no longer pressed down on her. Wishing she could tap into his mood, she again tried to free her arms. Maybe she wasn't ready to put an end to things, after all.

"I'm well aware that it feels strange," he said. "Get used to having only limited control over your body. I'm going to get you up and on your feet so you can have the maximum experience."

Giving her no time to process his words, he grabbed her shoulders and hauled her off the couch. He supported her as she planted her feet under her, even helped her stand.

Then he stepped away. Her elbows were so close together that her breasts were thrust out. Her arms flopped like useless appendages. She could move her fingers, not that it did her any good.

Dragging her attention off the in-control man who'd done this to her, she glanced over her shoulders but couldn't see his handiwork. It didn't matter. She knew.

"This," he said, "makes you more malleable."

"Malleable?" she shot back. "You — untie me!"

"No."

She should've demanded that he tell her when this *thing*

would end but she was in no position to argue with him. In truth, she was in no position to do anything.

He never took his gaze off her as he slowly circled. At first, she turned so she could keep watching him. Then she decided he was testing her nerves and stood with her head high and legs slightly spread to keep from swaying. Because the windows were open, heat and humidity, as well as the incessant insect humming and an overpowering smell, surrounded her. Maybe she could twist open the door and run outside, but he'd undoubtedly catch her and haul her back inside. Besides, she might lose her balance and fall down the stairs.

Might anger him.

If she hadn't worked so hard to make her independent way in the world, she would have already insisted on being rescued. But she was who she was, a woman who stood on her own two feet.

Usually.

Contemplating how much she'd lost, thanks to a single rope, briefly distracted her from him. Then he planted himself in front of her. He was so close his presence invaded her pores.

"I would have made a good hunter, a warrior," he informed her. "Valuable to the tribe."

"What am I? Some game you've shot?"

The moment the words were out of her mouth, she guessed she'd said the wrong thing, but was anything right? He clamped his fingers around her chin and forced her head up. When she tried to shake loose of his grip, he tightened his hold. Unnerved, she held still.

"I'd never shoot you. If you learn nothing else today, don't forget this. Part of my intention is to take you deep into yourself. I don't want to harm you. I know what I'm doing. I've always known…"

His silence added to her agitation, making it even more difficult for her to stand her ground. After what might've been the better part of a minute, he let go and walked over to the closest window. His back was to her, as if she no longer mattered to him.

What are you thinking?

"Did you have to do what you did?" Her voice trembled a little. "You must know I want to find out if I have a submissive side. I would have agreed to—"

He whirled around. "I don't care." He thumped his chest. "Right now is about me, examining *my* needs and seeing whether they've changed."

If it wasn't for his intense stare she would have questioned him about his needs, but the longer he regarded her, the less she wanted to know what was going on inside him. She considered herself a good judge of people and lack of turnover among her employees bore that out. Why, then, couldn't she begin to grasp what her captor was about?

Listen and learn. And don't push him.

The corner of his mouth twitched. "Turn around. I want to see what you look like helpless."

He'd already done that, not that she was in any position to argue the point. As she swiveled away from him, she tried bringing her arms closer together, to see if she could make the rope slide off her, but the strands remained snugly in place. Her arms were starting to numb while the ache between her shoulder blades was hard to ignore.

Not pain, she acknowledged when her back was to him. Another sensation, more intimate.

Wondering if his intention was to make her admit he'd turned her on a little, she again faced him.

"I used to Dom here every free minute I had," he told her. "I know how addictive the lifestyle can become. For some people, the need explodes the first moment they experience it. Others need a slow immersion. I exploded. I'll soon learn which it is for you."

Not sure she fully grasped what he'd told her, she opted to wait and see if he'd continue. Thinking back over some of the things he'd said, she realized he'd spoken of his needs, not hers.

The walls seemed to be drawing toward her, undoubtedly a by-product of being trapped in the room with him. She told herself it was better this way when he went over to one of the wicker chairs and sat. At the same time, she felt even more exposed.

He leaned forward, lifted the lid on the chest and extracted a pair of scissors.

Chapter Six

"What's that for?" she blurted. "You can't cut—"

"I've already demonstrated I can do whatever I want. Maybe I'll hack off your hair, including what's hiding your pussy."

His hands on her pussy, drawing out her flesh so he could see what he was doing. Maybe, first, tying her down so she couldn't move. A long, hot shudder ran through her.

"Trying to wrap your mind around that, are you?" He opened and closed the shining blades. "It won't be the last time I throw possibilities at you. The thing is, you won't know which I intend to make good on until I start."

Fighting to hold his threat at bay, she straightened. When had she started to slump? Certainly, she wasn't already admitting defeat. "You're trying to scare me."

"Is it working?"

Head still high, she shook it.

"I don't believe you." He jabbed a finger at the floor in front of him. "Kneel here."

Where's the damned listening device? If it worked as well as she'd been assured of, someone was listening to every word being said. Obviously, he didn't care.

Fine. Neither did she. Yet.

"I gave you an order," he snapped. "Kneel here."

"No." Where had the denial come from?

"Oh?" He flexed the fingers of the hand not holding the scissors. "Do you really think you can make good on that?"

Remember what you are, a tough broad. "I deserve to know what I'm getting into. Maybe I'll decide to stop working with you, select someone more—"

"That isn't up to you."

She was in over her head with this man. He knew how to fuck with her mind and was, probably, just getting started.

Where would he take her? Was there another existence for her at the end of this journey, a place of peace and acceptance, a willingness to let him dominate every aspect of her existence?

She could either let him walk her down that dark road or fight. In the end, the result might be the same — if it was that simple.

There was too much to think about, too many options that weren't because he'd drawn her elbows together.

"I'm confusing you. Good, because that's my intention." He slid the scissors over the mound between his legs. "I take pride in a certain element of self-control. At least I have that. I can, and often do put off achieving sexual satisfaction until I'm convinced the sub has earned this." He repeated the gesture. "Until you beg for it."

She'd concluded forced sex would be part of her indoctrination into submission and had wondered what would tip her so far over the edge that she'd want to be taken. What she hadn't prepared for was to have the challenge thrown out so soon.

"I'm not a nympho, so if you're expecting —"

"I told you, I have no preconceived notions about who and what you are. Down on your knees with your back to me."

Warm air from the overhead fan brushed her cheeks and throat. He was waiting for her to make the next move, which, in turn, would dictate what he did next. She debated refusing, but if she did now, she'd have drawn a line in the sand when she had to discover how far he intended to take her.

Wondering what had happened to the independent woman she'd always believed she was, she awkwardly sank down facing him. Her knees struck the hard floor and she started to tip forward. "Damn." As the stinging sensation in her knees subsided, she studied the floor. It was spotless.

"I'm waiting."

I know you are. I just – Cutting off what would have been an excuse, she turned in a half-circle until she was staring at the closed door, beyond which waited what might dictate how she lived the rest of her life. She was aware of every inch of her body, mostly her shoulders, arms and back. Undoubtedly, he was staring at that part of her knowing she couldn't see him.

A whispery sound caught her attention. By the time she realized he'd stood, he was pressing his hand against the back of her head. Unable to resist, she fell forward. He grabbed her hair and eased her down the last few inches. Her forehead was on the floor, her nose so close she could smell the varnished wood.

"What the hell?" She tried to sit up.

He flattened his hand over her head and easily kept her in place.

"I could have given you more precise directions like I did before, but sometimes I opt for physically demonstrating control. This is one of those times. You are not to move." He thumped the top of her head. "Got it. Stay where you belong."

Where I belong? Like some animal on a short leash?

Tears stung her eyes. Grateful for the curtain of her hair, she blinked the moisture away. No matter what happened, she would not cry.

"Clothes have no business in here, at least for you. I want to see what I got for my troubles."

Her lower arms had fallen forward enough that she might've been able to plant her hands on the floor and keep some of the pressure off her forehead. No matter that she must've looked foolish, she'd take what little self-determination she could.

In a moment.

He started walking around her, his sandals slapping against wood. She hated bowing before him and yet – and yet the newness stroked her. It was so simple for him to turn her into something she'd never imagined becoming.

Warm fingers slid under the bottom of her shorts. He raked his nails over the backs of her thighs, making her jump and whimper.

"That's the sound," he muttered. "One I intend to hear many times a day. Focus on the sensation. That's the only thing you have to do."

When he scratched her again, she started to yelp. Afraid of angering him, she clenched her teeth. His nails were thick but thankfully not sharp. As he repeatedly marked her, she struggled to take his suggestion to heart. The stinging, biting sensations became her everything. She dismissed the imprisoning rope and barely noticed the blood that had rushed to her head. This nameless man was attacking her thighs and buttocks, not causing pain as much as introducing her to something without beginning or end.

This moment was everything, the sum and substance of her existence. Anticipating every sharp stroke, feeling the tingling ease, only to roar back.

"Good," he muttered. "Good. Stay with it. Claim the pain."

Pain?

Before she could think what to do with the word, he yanked down on her shorts and slapped her ass. Hard.

"What the—? Damn it, what are you doing?"

Maybe she'd tried to straighten, because he planted a hand over the back of her head and pushed down.

"Shut the fuck up."

To some extent she'd known he'd been toying with her. His outburst shocked her into obeying.

He slapped her buttocks again. Anticipating yet another blow, she tensed. When it didn't immediately come, she imagined he was laughing at her. Maybe that was better than dealing with his temper.

A third slap, this one even harder, knocked her off her knees and forward onto the floor. Ignoring her half-off shorts, she squirmed around until she could see him.

"I sometimes block out my actions," he told her. "Doing so keeps me in the real world." He paused. "Other times the situation plays itself out." He jerked his head at the scissors. "Get your ass in the air again. If you don't, I'll spank you."

Spank me? She tried to acknowledge his warning but her mind balked. One thing she had no doubt of, this wasn't an idle threat. In addition, his expression was becoming darker. She repeatedly struggled to hoist herself off the floor but kept failing until she hit upon rolling onto her back and sitting up, using her hands to brace herself. She tucked her knees under her, rocked onto them, and straightened. Then, because the job was only half-done, she leaned forward so her temple once more pressed against the floor. The life she'd lived before now faded to nothing.

"Good body tone," he observed from behind her. "I'm going to enjoy challenging you."

For how long, she needed to know, but asking would have to wait.

Her shorts only covered the bottom half of her buttocks. As she readied herself for more scratching or a continuation of being spanked, she felt less than she'd been when she'd started toward the island a lifetime ago.

Not yet something new.

When he grabbed her shorts waistband, it took her a moment to realize he was putting the cotton under tension so the scissors could more easily slice through the fabric. He started at the bottom hem and marched slowly, steadily toward her waist. She'd never imagined scissors could be so strong. When he was done, he drew the severed fabric away from her hip until it hung. She was still wearing her panties and the other side of her shorts was in place.

Not for long.

No matter that she wasn't sure she was ready for this, she mentally followed what he was doing as he repeated the action on the other side of her shorts. What had adequately covered her not long ago now dangled. She brought her legs together in an attempt to keep the ruined garment on her.

"No," he said.

Too much blood pulsed in her forehead, making her slow to comprehend what he had in mind as he rammed his hand between her legs and forced them apart. He grabbed the loose material and yanked down.

"Done." He draped the garment over the back of her neck. "Obviously, you aren't going to have any more use for that. Ever. Now, what next?"

Let me go! Keep me here!

He ran his fingers into her hair and used it as a handle to straighten her. That done, he closed his hand around the elbow rope and hauled her to her feet, standing as he did.

"I don't believe in wasting time. Some Doms prefer the slow start, but I'm not one of them. Not anymore. Stay right there. I need to make some modifications."

Fear had a life of its own, a will stronger than her determination not to let it win. No matter that he didn't want her to move, she couldn't stop herself from looking over her shoulder as he dug into the chest again. When he took out another length of rope and looped it over the back of his neck, she wondered if she'd always dread what the chest contained. At least he hadn't chosen handcuffs or a whip.

Whip?

Yes, eventually.

Red! Red!

No. Not yet.

Chapter Seven

He grabbed her upper arms and marched her across the room, stopping when he'd shoved her against the closed door to what she assumed was the bedroom. When he let go, she knew not to move.

"The wind is increasing," he whispered. "The trees are waving, bending, surrendering to a greater power. I know what that's like."

Alerted by his new tone, she searched her mind for something to say that might take her closer to understanding him. "How does that make you feel?" she finally came up with.

"Lost," he muttered. "Helpless."

Deeply shaken, she looked behind her. For maybe two seconds, their gazes locked, but she couldn't see beneath the surface.

"You, helpless?" She swallowed. "That's what I should be saying."

"What?" He shook his head. "Damn it, I don't want you moving. Get back into position."

Even as she stared ahead of her, she vowed not to let another opportunity to get to know the man beneath the surface escape her. She heard him breathing, the sounds harsh, as if he'd been exerting himself. Finally, his breaths slowed and quieted.

"There are obvious drawbacks to the way I've restrained you." His tone was back to normal. "For one, the longer the rope remains in place, the more feeling you're going to lose in your arms." He massaged the back of her neck. "There is one advantage, at least for me. Can you fathom what it is?"

"No."

"It's easier to control you."

"Easier than this? What more do you want?"

She expected punishment. Hell, maybe she'd deliberately prodded him to see how he'd react.

"It'll come," he muttered.

"What will come?"

"Your acceptance. And pleasure."

He wasn't making sense, not that she was in any position to call it to his attention. She vowed to not say or do anything to antagonize him so maybe he'd relax. "I like the pleasure part."

"I know."

"Is that because all the women you've worked with are the same? How many have there been?"

He shoved her aside and opened the door. "No more talking, slave. Get in there."

'Slave'. The word snaked through her like something alive, and she barely paid attention to where she was going as he propelled her into the next room. Unlike the living room, the windows in this one were high and small. She glimpsed the sky and the tops of wildly gyrating trees. He'd been right, this was no gentle wind.

A queen-sized bed had been positioned near the middle of the room but that wasn't what captured her attention. The space was a bondage playground, complete with a seven-foot-high metal 'X', chains hanging from the ceiling, and a wooden armchair with a hole where the seat should've been. Imagining what the box on the floor under the chair seat contained started her shivering all over again. A second wooden storage container had been placed against the wall to the left of the door.

Safe, she forcefully reminded herself. She was safe here.

Unless he got lost.

"The door locks from the outside," he informed her. "I have the key."

Of course he did. And he'd undoubtedly never let her

forget it.

"First things first," he continued from behind her. "Making you more comfortable."

She jumped when he crossed one wrist over the other, but didn't try to pull away. His finger felt so good, caressing and demanding at the same time. When he started looping the soft rope around her wrists, she drew a mental image of what he was doing. He was creating a multi-strand 'X' she'd never be able to get out of on her own and yet the blood flow wasn't being cut off.

What was wrong with her? Shouldn't she be protesting she'd had enough, that she'd changed her mind and wanted to go back to the life she knew?

No.

"This, too, will change." He took hold of her wrists and lifted them, so she had no choice but to lean forward. After a pause, he continued. "My intention is to introduce you to the variety of positions I'll put you into over the course of our time together." He let go, allowing her to straighten. "This is just an example, a taste. From now on, you'll always be restrained in one way or another. Freedom no longer has meaning to you."

No longer free.

His captive.

His slave.

Wet heat filled her pussy. Shocked and excited, she fought the need to clench her inner muscles so, hopefully, he wouldn't know everything about her. Determined to hold on to the sensation, she closed her eyes. Maybe she was a sick bitch, a nympho who'd been waiting her entire life for these moments. Oh, she knew he was deliberately testing her with words and actions, but she'd signed up for this and, by God, she was going to milk it for all it was worth.

As long as she could handle it.

"No objections?" he asked as he let go and, once more, rested his hands on her shoulders. "You didn't say anything about my calling you a slave."

"No." She gave herself a mental shake and tried again. "I didn't."

"We'll take another look at that later, but first things first."

When his hands left her shoulders, fear that he intended to leave her locked in the room like this killed some of her sexual excitement. She didn't trust herself not to beg him to stay with her. Then she realized he was releasing the rope on her elbows. The pins and needles sensation increased until she couldn't hold back a moan.

"Learn to deal with it," he said to her as he massaged her arms. "Discomfort is part of the experience."

Every nerve in her upper body felt inflamed, yet she willed herself to stand in place. It hadn't taken him long to demonstrate his mastery over her body. She likened herself to a wild filly that had been roped and dragged into a corral. However, unlike the panicked animal, she lived for every experience.

She wanted this. Needed ropes on her wrists, her shorts slashed, his hands easing away the discomfort he was responsible for. She even needed his moments of darkness.

"Better?" he asked.

"Better."

"Thank me."

She filled her lungs. "Thank you."

"Not enough." Using the rope on her wrists, he again forced her to lean over. "What's my name, slave?"

I don't know. "Master." The word exploded from her. "Master."

"That's what I wanted to hear, but you don't really believe it, not yet." He forced her arms even higher so she was in danger of toppling. "Not yet."

He started marching her forward, forcing her to concentrate on every step. All too soon they reached the bed. The plush white coverlet seemed new. Despite what was happening to her, she wondered who'd made the bed and what that person had been thinking while he or she had been at work.

A hard shove between her shoulder blades sent her head first into the clean-smelling cover. She turned her head to the side so she could breathe and made no attempt to straighten. The bed was waist-high. Her buttocks were on display, inches from his hands.

"Time to get a better look at the merchandise," he informed her as he gripped her panties waistband. "I want to see what I'll be working with."

He started tugging the flimsy garment over her ass cheeks, making the journey slow, taking her with it. Goosebumps dotted her newly exposed flesh. Instead of finishing the task, so she was naked from the waist down, he left her panties bunched around her thighs.

"Spread your legs, slave. Show your Master what you have for him."

Wait a minute! I'm not sure I want to be treated this way.

He slapped her left cheek with enough force to send her upper body sliding over the bed so her head hung off the side. "Shut up!" A second blow landed, this one on her right cheek. It stung. A lot.

"Damn it!" she blurted. "What the hell —?"

"One more outburst and I'll gag you. You have so much to learn, starting and ending with understanding who owns you."

As he continued spanking her, something shifted, an opening of an inner door. The energy exiting him and entering her said this was no game to him. He wasn't some for-hire Dom brought in to fulfill a role for MSDB. Who he'd been before coming here today no longer existed.

Might never return.

And that made him dangerous.

Possibly deadly.

Red?

The blows became a storm, a battering of her senses that killed the question of whether to admit she'd had enough. A fierce burning sensation spread out until she was on fire from the middle of her back to her calves. Self-preservation instinct kicked in, causing her to try to escape the sensual yet harsh attack, but as she wrenched to the left or right or tried to straighten, he remained one step ahead of her. Her ability to think and plan splintered until only the desperate need to comprehend remained.

She sobbed, cursed, ducked her head and gnawed at the expensive fabric he'd imprisoned her against. Sweat bloomed everywhere as she fought her useless fight.

He was tireless, his hands delivering relentless punishment she didn't deserve but had to tolerate. The longer he spanked her, the more she accepted what he was doing.

Bottom line—he was in control. He'd punish her for as long and in every way he wanted.

Fire! All-consuming fire. Body flying apart, splintering, shredding.

Wonderfully so.

He rammed first one leg then the other between hers, forcing her to widen her stance as much as the nylon roping her thighs allowed. When he stopped spanking her and clamped his powerful fingers over her ass cheeks, her back ached.

"Stay with the sensations." He squeezed the inflamed flesh. "Feel it everywhere."

Of course she did. It wasn't as if she had a choice—or wanted anything else.

Her clamped buttocks belonged to him, acted as a conduit to every part of her but, mostly, her mind. The longer he held her in this strange new way, the harder it was to remember she was a separate human being. She wasn't in over her head as much as trapped in a new experience.

"I could fuck you just like this," he informed her. "Wait. Let me rephrase that. I *will* fuck you, but only when you beg me to."

'*Beg*'? Maybe. Anything was possible.

"Maybe you're trying to figure out how to tell me to go to hell and make it stand for something. Is that what you're doing?"

This man who'd upended her world was asking a question, but how to answer?

"Opportunity lost."

Wait! He hadn't given her enough time.

She was still trying to pull her thoughts together when he released her throbbing buttocks. Undoubtedly, he'd left indentations on her soft flesh.

"Time for a lesson in what happens to slaves who can't keep up with the program. Hopefully, this will impress you with the importance of putting my wishes first. If it doesn't, I'll design something else."

Threat or promise? If only she dared ask.

A clicking from behind her sent her heart into overdrive. She tried to tell herself he was deliberately testing her sanity, but what good did it do when he was a master at it? Her already taut panties pressed even tighter against her thighs.

"What—?" she started.

"Shut up." He jerked on the nylon. "You'll find out soon enough."

What did he mean? He might, occasionally, offer an explanation but mostly he expected her to learn from experience. She'd bury herself in her education and become an expert in a something she only dimly grasped.

The clicking repeated. She concentrated on trying to make sense of it, but by the time she realized he'd been opening and closing the scissors, he'd started attacking her panties. He severed them as he had her shorts and pulled the worthless fabric off her. She thought he'd loop it over the back of her neck like before. Instead, he grabbed a hank of her hair and lifted her head.

"Open your mouth," he ordered. "I'm going to gag you."

Wait! she nearly yelled. If he did, she wouldn't be able to call for help.

Silenced, she'd have no choice but to take the next step.

Chapter Eight

Not waiting to see if she'd obey, the man pressed the sex-juice-scented panties against her lips. Distracted by the pain in her scalp, she opened her mouth. He filled it with nylon then let go of her hair.

Her head dropped and she focused on trying to swallow around the wad. She could've spat it out, but he'd have shoved it back in and maybe run tape over her lips. She'd complied, not because she wanted to be silenced, maybe, but this way she could scream into the gag if things became more than she could handle.

She'd been mugged several years before. The bastard who'd knocked her down had gotten away with her purse and less than twenty dollars. He's also left her with bruises, plus a fear of being caught unawares she hadn't completely gotten over.

This was much worse so why wasn't she afraid?

Why did she want to see what he had in mind for her first lesson?

"You *will* remain in this position while I gather what I need." He punctuated his command by swatting the backs of both thighs. Her pussy clenched.

It took a moment for her to realize he'd left her. At first, she couldn't think beyond the delicious warmth inside her but, as the seconds stretched out, her awareness of the rest of her body increased. She was still dressed — at least she was on top. In telling contrast, he'd stripped off everything except her sandals from the waist down. Her buttocks still burned. When she replayed what he'd done to make them feel that way, her muscles tightened again.

She didn't want to be positioned like this, damn it. What self-respecting woman would want her pale, naked ass waving in the air? If anyone came in, they'd see her reddened buttocks and spread legs. More telling, her cunt was on display.

Juices trickling down the insides of her thighs.

Groaning into the gag that carried the taste of her arousal, she acknowledged she was turned on.

Eager for his return.

Needing his cock inside her.

He grabbed her left ankle, lifted her leg and pulled off her sandal. She told herself she wanted nothing to do with this.

Wanted the hell out.

After removing her other sandal, he kicked at the insides of both ankles, forcing her to open her stance even more. She never shaved her pussy hair, in part because she had so little of it. It seemed like too much work, and she didn't want her infrequent sex partners jumping to any conclusions.

What did *Master* think of what he was seeing?

Maybe he'd demand she denude herself there.

Maybe he'd do the job.

An image of her sprawled and restrained on a medical examination table while he approached with a safety razor stripped some of the air from the room. She hadn't really meant it when she'd called him 'Master'. Now, it was too late to take back the word.

Maybe it was the truth—would become her reality.

After depositing something on the bed near her hips, he took hold of them and drew her toward him until her legs dangled and her feet brushed the floor. Without his legs bracing her, she'd slide off.

"What brought you here?" He ground something—it felt like his knee—against her crotch. "You can't answer, so it's up to me to figure it out. Hell." His breath escaped in a rush. "Hell, I don't know what compels me to do some of the things I do, so how can I—? Someone on the outside knows you're here. You aren't stupid enough to turn yourself over

54

to MSDB without having a safety net. What is it, a time limit? You've told your contact to call the cops if you don't return in X number of hours?"

She couldn't focus on what he was saying, not with his knee grinding against her over-sensitive flesh.

"Hopefully, you're smart enough to see the flaw in that." He slid both hands under her top. His thumbs settled over her spine. "Where will your friend tell the cops to look? It'll take them a long time to search all the islands. MSDB has set up a number of systems to ensure—never mind."

No, not 'never mind'. She needed to hear more about those systems.

As if he'd tell her.

"Have you ever seen a horse being broken?" His thumbs began a slow march up and down her spinal column. "There are several ways of doing it, some traumatic for the animal, some gentle. The end result is basically the same, an animal ready for human use."

Was he saying he intended to break her? That wasn't right. She hadn't come here to—

"Some trainers don't care what the experience is like for the animal, but I need to. I must..."

His touch was softening her, taking her to a place she'd never been. His heartbeat pulsed in his thumbs, left him and entered her backbone. It didn't matter that she knew nothing about him. Let him liken her to a bronc. As long as his life force continued its slow slide into her, she—what?

Her panties seemed to be swelling. If that continued, she'd gag on them. Determined to take her thoughts back to what this domineering man was doing to her, she worked a little of the fabric out of her mouth. Hopefully, with her head down, he wouldn't see what she'd done.

Wouldn't disapprove or think he needed to punish her.

"It's complex." He'd been silent long enough that his voice caught her off balance. "Multi-layered when I need it simple."

He planted his palms over her shoulder blades and

pressed down, sealing her to the bed. Her bounds arms were deeply bent, her bare legs spread wide.

"MSDB rules stipulate that the client's needs come first." He grunted. "Everything for the paying customer. Nothing for the man who makes the experience possible."

Was he complaining about his employer and, if so, did he expect her to do something about it? Darn it, wasn't everything going his way? He could do whatever he wanted to her like unzip himself and —

"You don't want to hear this," he muttered. "Hell, I don't want to talk about it."

His weight continued to hold her in place, but it was getting easier to breathe. Being mugged had been a terrifying experience, in large part because it had been so unexpected. In contrast, she'd gone into today with her eyes open — at least, she'd thought she'd known what she'd signed up for.

It hadn't been this.

Or had it?

She flexed her ankles, pushed her toes against the floor and lifted her buttocks maybe an inch. Even as she tried to make her peace with the sex-starved woman who was doing this thing, she prayed he'd noticed. When he didn't react, she struggled to free herself from the bed but couldn't, thanks to his weight, his all-commanding weight. His slipped his hands from her shoulders to her waist, burning her as he traveled.

"Training fascinates me," he said. "The deep, get-it-done process of fashioning a person into something new. A just-broken horse tolerates being ridden. Maybe he figures it's a fair trade for regular hay and water, but in his heart of hearts he still longs to run free. That's not what I intend to do with you."

You want to alter my reality so I won't think to fight your ropes.

Her thoughts swirled until she could barely concentrate on what was happening. Every time she tried to imagine herself holding up her hands for binding, however, her mind balked. This was all too new, with too much happening. Eyes closed, she took stock of her body, from her cheek against the satiny spread, to Master's knee sealed against her crotch. There wasn't an inch of her he didn't impact, a breath she took that didn't include his essence.

"Enough. I have no intention of revealing anything about myself."

But he already had. She just didn't know how to process the little she'd learned.

One, then two arms slipped between her waist and the bed. He lifted her off it and pulled her back against him, not stopping until his erection was mashed between them and grinding into the small of her back. Her fingers hummed with the desire to capture his cock while instinct warned her not to try.

After all, he was the one in charge.

"Spit out the gag," he ordered. "I'm going to ask some questions."

And she would answer as honestly as possible, she decided as she pushed out the sex-tasting garment. It briefly hung up on her chin then fell to the bed.

"Done," she announced around her humming, ever-heating body.

"Yeah. I know."

Wondering if she'd done something wrong by speaking without permission, she struggled to focus on anything other than her naked body and the masculine form behind her. He wrapped one arm around her breasts and the other over her waist. The longer she stood there without use of her hands the righter it felt. This way, he made all the decisions and moves. All she had to do was react.

React, yes. Feel, yes.

He took one deep breath after another. Her thoughts followed the act. What was it she'd concluded, that he outweighed her by about a hundred pounds? He was nearly twice as big as she was, which made him doubly intimidating.

Arousing to the max.

His muscled forearm flattened her breasts. He seemed to be everywhere and everything, all-consuming. Hungry cock grinding against her. Light-headed from the overload of sensation, she arched her back and pushed her buttocks toward him. Two could do this thing, this sexual dance of desire and anticipation.

Maybe she held the upper hand after all.

Her self-confidence and need for adventure growing, she leaned into him. "This feels good," she admitted. "Damn good. What—what happens next?"

He sucked in air, one deep breath after another, making her dizzy from the effort. If asked, she wouldn't have been able to describe the room. How could her surroundings matter when her body was marching down a road she hadn't known existed?

When only the journey mattered.

"You're asking what happens next?" he ground out. "You want an outline?"

She'd displeased him in some way, but how could she determine what that was when he'd given her so little?

"I didn't mean— You said you wanted to ask me some questions."

More deep breathing on his part followed her comment. Maybe he wasn't as self-contained as she'd initially believed. She'd come into this—this situation believing she could trust whoever was in charge of her 'education' to run every aspect of the show. That was how she'd wanted it.

He released her, not giving her time to prepare before shoving her against the bed. She struck it first with her breasts, followed by her chin. Angry and startled, she planted her feet under her and pushed off it. To her surprise, he made no attempt to force her down again. Her back was to him so she could only guess what he was doing. One thing she knew—the item he'd placed on the bed was a vibrator.

Vibrators brought pleasure. And climaxes.

Shivering, she swiveled and faced him. He didn't so much as blink as he perched on the seat-less chair.

"Right there." He jabbed a finger at a spot some two feet in front of him. "Stand there."

Instead of making a run for the door, she did as he'd commanded. His hard stare made her even more aware of her half-naked state.

What was the point of still wearing a bra and T-shirt when she was nude from the waist down? Someone who didn't know what this was about might've concluded she'd stopped in the middle of getting dressed. That person might've wondered why she hadn't put on her panties before slipping into the pale yellow top she had no use for on a worksite, but maybe he — of course it would be a he — wouldn't care.

"Tell me something," he said. "The things I've done so far, the bound wrists and getting rid of your panties and shorts, how does that make you feel?"

Master got right to the point. She'd be wise not to forget that.

She dug her toes into the carpet. "Awkward."

He shook his head. "Damn it, you can do better."

She hadn't given him enough. Fighting the piercing glare of his gaze, she looked down at herself. Her breasts hindered her view somewhat, but she could and did fill in the spaces.

"I'm sorry, but I'm in uncharted waters."

"Why did you decide to come here?"

Momentary relief at not having to answer his earlier question faded as she realized he'd asked an even harder one. At the moment, she was taller than him which, maybe, should have increased her self-confidence but didn't. The longer she was with him, the more his presence impacted her. Women wouldn't consider him handsome but neither could they dismiss him. He controlled not just the cabin's doors, but the air in here. His unrelenting gaze cut through her layers.

She licked her lips. "Even before I learned about the MSDB site, I was questioning certain elements of my existence."

"You're too young for a mid-life crisis."

"It isn't that." She shook her head then cast around for what she should say next. She'd always been the quiet one in her family, more comfortable doing than talking. "I have a business that sucks up nearly all of my time. When I was trying to get it off the ground, the only thing that mattered was being able to pay the bills."

Were his eyes glazing? Maybe this wasn't what he wanted to hear. Unsure of how to proceed, she slid one foot then the other over the floor.

"Why landscaping? That's a man's career."

"Says who?" she snapped. "Granted, I can't compete with the big boys, but my customers don't give a damn about my gender, as long as I complete a job on time and on budget, which I've done ninety-nine percent of the time."

His mouth twitched, the gesture telling her his intention had been to push her buttons.

"Why are we talking about this?" she asked. "I thought — I paid for a sexual experience."

He stretched out his legs. "Is that the only thing you paid for?"

She closed her mouth. Everything had changed. She'd never so much as imagined an experience like this, but here she was. She'd be crazy not to live this new reality to the fullest.

To try to learn more about herself.

"I don't fit in a box. My family — I have two older brothers and am close to all four of my male cousins — saw me as a tomboy. I wanted to be included in what they did. Maybe that's why my feminine potential…"

At a loss for words, she tore her attention from the man she'd called Master and took note of the tree tops just beyond her existence. They continued their wild, disjointed dance. In some respects, the trees were like her, trapped by a greater force.

"Go on."

Snagged by the low voice, she faced the nameless man again. His casual stance might've deceived other people, but she could see beneath the surface to where coiled energy throbbed. The backs of his knuckles on the wooden chair arms had turned white. His chest rose and fell, rose and fell while his gray eyes continued their relentless probing.

Go deep into yourself, they demanded. Maybe he was speaking to both of them.

"I don't know how to be feminine." She stuck out a foot that had never had a massage or pedicure. "I own one dress and my makeup—I've been out of lipstick for weeks."

His attention moved from her to what was taking place outside. Something seemed to be changing about him, a growing hardness perhaps. *Is it getting darker in here?* Maybe a storm was approaching. If that were the case, she might be trapped with him until it was over.

More trapped than she already was.

"If you want to play to your feminine side," he said, "why don't you?"

"I didn't say that."

"Didn't you?"

"No," she insisted, then remained silent.

His eyes were definitely duskier than when she'd first spotted him, and the fine lines at his lips were more prominent. He reminded her of a guard dog she'd considered buying but hadn't because she'd sensed she wouldn't be able to control it. The difference between then and now was that the dog had been chained up while this man was free to—to attack her if he wanted.

If the impulse became more than he could resist.

"What about you?" she asked. "What brought you here? What do you get out of your association with MSDB?"

He straightened, prompting her to slide back a few inches.

"Don't," he commanded. "Stay where you are."

Or what?

"I don't understand you." She leveled him with a stare

that came from years of being the boss. "If this is your way of trying to fuck with my mind, I don't appreciate it."

A slow shrug rippled through his upper body. "Tell someone who cares. As for not understanding me, that's exactly what I want."

"I'm sure it is."

The ghost of a smile eased his features, followed by a return to stern remoteness. A man whose 'work' called for assuming a Dom role should've enjoyed what he was doing, shouldn't he? After all, sex was a major part of the job's perks, and what male didn't want that?

"So you were, what, a jock while you were growing up?" he asked.

She rolled her shoulders. "Kind of. I'd rather do something physical and nothing pleased me more than digging in the dirt." She glanced at the window. The trees lashed about. "Seeing if I can make things grow."

"Grow."

The rumbling word pulled her attention back to him. He was looking not at but through her, his mind somewhere else. "What is it?" she asked. "What—?"

"Don't!" He clenched his jaw. "I was talking, damn it, learning more about you."

"Were you?"

"Yes. Gardening is a form of nurturing, a trait people associate with the female sex. Just because you don't wear pink or false lashes doesn't make you any less a woman."

Was that a compliment? Maybe that was his off-handed way of pointing out her half-naked state. One thing she did know—as long as she stood before him like this she was hard-pressed to carry on a conversation, let alone try to grasp what was taking place inside him.

He blinked. "When and how did you lose your virginity?"

"What? I thought we were talking about—?"

He started rubbing the chair arms. "About dirt and growing things, no. Answer the damn question."

So much for thinking there was anything approaching

equality between them. She was no longer as aroused as she'd been when he'd dispensed with half of her clothes, but the question took her a step in that direction. Of course he'd insist on keeping the discussion about sexual matters. The bit about gardening had been to knock her off balance.

Besides, sex was what she wanted, wasn't it?

"I lost my virginity during my senior year of high school." She felt herself being pulled into the past. "A group of us were at a party. There was drinking and making out. I-I hadn't done much of either. The music was like drumbeats and the heat — the air was close and hot and alive."

"You got drunk?"

She'd told a few girlfriends about the first time, so it wasn't as if she hadn't been down this road, but she'd been among friends then. Not standing with her legs clamped together in a vain attempt to prevent a stranger from seeing her sex, and her hands helpless behind her.

"High, not drunk. Feeling things I wasn't handling well because boys kept brushing against my breasts or grabbing my ass."

"Come closer." He spread his legs. "Turn around."

Chapter Nine

Reminding herself that part of why she'd paid for this adventure was to hear words like those, she settled herself between his thighs and presented him with her rear end. Restlessness again claimed her.

"So the boys were doing this?" He ran a nail down her right butt cheek.

"No," she whimpered, struggling to remain in place with her legs together.

"Maybe this, then?" He raked her left cheek.

"No." She tried to tuck her buttocks under her. "It wasn't—"

"I don't care." He grabbed both cheeks and squeezed them.

Her spine straightened then arched of its own accord. Her fingers curled inward so her nails dug into her palms. If she wasn't careful she'd fall forward, which would place her even more at his mercy—not that mercy was part of him.

The pressure let up but nothing about his hold said he might release her. "Am I getting warmer or colder with regard to the night of your unflowering?"

Don't play along. Maybe that way he'll relent. "I was dressed back then."

"What were you wearing?"

"Jeans," she blurted, because she'd seldom worn anything else.

"Tight ones that cupped you like this?" Discomfort oozed out of her beat by beat as his fingers cradled her ass. "Snug jeans designed to drive horny teenage boys crazy."

"I didn't—" Her memory of that night was foggy, but

she'd known there weren't going to be any adults at the house. One of her few girlfriends — she tended to hang out with the boys in Future Farmers — had begged her to go with her because, as her friend had said, everyone except the geeks would be there.

She'd agreed, not just to keep her friend company, but because something had been humming inside her for months.

"I don't like having to remind my sex slaves to be honest." He hoisted her cheeks higher. "Finish, damn it."

'Sex slave'? Harsh energy drove through her. Despite the heady sensations, however, being half-dressed was a confusing experience. She didn't know whether to embrace her partial nudity or focus on her top and bra. One thing she was certain of, she wanted him to call her 'slave' again.

Despite her heated thoughts, she stumbled through a description of that night. At first, the girlfriend she'd gone to the party with had stayed by her side while they'd dealt with their nerves by grading the boys' appearance. Most had been physically unfinished, more children than men, but a few had crossed over. With two beers fueling her imagination, she'd started her own scoring system. Brad's voice had dropped and he'd probably shaved several times a week, but his shoulders had been narrow. The Hendley twins had been well over six feet tall. Their hands had been big, their hips narrow and the width of their shoulders — just studying them had dampened her panties. They'd played football, basketball and baseball, which had made them jocks to the max.

Unfortunately, they'd had eyes only for the cheerleaders.

"Then Jake handed me a bottle," she told the commanding man behind her. "Until then, I'd thought of him as my brother's friend."

"Something shifted inside you."

Master still had hold of her buttocks but he'd simply cradled them as she spun out her story. She'd been able to think and speak around the sensation.

"I guess," she admitted.

"You guess?" His grip tightened, became almost painful.

"No." She hated her whimpering tone. "Something changed in me that moment. Jake kept his hands on the bottle longer than necessary and looked at me in a way that made me feel like — like a deer in the headlights."

"You liked the sensation."

"Yes."

"Something a woman and not a child feels."

Before she could admit he was right, he stood, grabbed her tethered wrists and pushed her arms up, forcing her to bend over. She felt her helplessness in every cell.

"Keep going."

You don't have to do this. "We went outside. He'd driven his older brother's truck." She had to work at not drooling, and speaking was hard.

"The cab or the bed?"

"The cab," she got out. "I wouldn't let him do it out where someone might see."

"His doing you? That's how you saw it?"

"I didn't know what I was supposed to do."

"Sounds like every girl's dream, sprawled out on a plastic seat with the steering wheel in the way. Was it as good as you thought it would be? Did you climax?"

The truth was she'd been so damned nervous he'd had to moisten her opening with his spit. The pain of that first penetration had sobered her. Jake had nearly come before he'd gotten all the way in. After, he'd patted her shoulder and thanked her. She'd put up with his awkward attempts to soothe her. Then she'd pulled her jeans back up and hurried into the house so she could clean up in the bathroom.

"I'm not going to say I'm sorry it turned out the way it did," he said, "because I'm not."

"I know."

He jerked her onto her feet and marched her back to the bed. Instead of forcing her onto it, he sat on the side and positioned her between his legs facing away from him. He slipped his hands into her hair and drew her head back a bit. That done, he snaked his other arm around her hips and cupped her mons.

Seconds marched past. The hold on her mons loosened. A low groan oozed from him. "No," she thought he said.

His breath dampened her head and shoulders. She couldn't make sense of what had just happened to him. "I asked why you'd signed up for a MSDB experience but I already know the answer," he said. "It's the same reason the other women I've worked with have. You need to give up control."

'Need'. She didn't do one-night stands. All right, she sometimes imagined what would happen if she walked into a dark bar and sized up the possibilities. Once she'd picked the most likely prospect, she'd offer to buy him a drink. The dance of suggestive words wouldn't last long. In minutes, they'd head for the nearest motel for a night of uninhibited fucking. Come morning, they'd go their separate ways.

Any chance of leaving today had been taken out of her hands. Even if this turned out to be a one-night stand, she'd never forget it.

"It's that simple?" she asked. "I have the money to indulge in some game playing and you're ready to take me up on it?"

"No, it isn't that simple."

Of course it wasn't. She was sorry she'd put it that way.

"I don't want to fight with you," she admitted. "You have me at a physical disadvantage."

"Yeah, I do."

She'd been careful to remain still through their exchange, but it was so damn hard. In contrast, the hand over her mons threatened to claim her full attention. His fingers had already twitched several times, as if foreshadowing what he intended to do next.

"I spend my days dealing with the law," he told her. "Everything I say, do or write is within the framework of our country's legal system. I know better than most the consequences of stepping outside that framework. I go after those arrogant or stupid enough to believe laws aren't for them. If they're stupid, I'm inclined to cut them more slack than someone who thumbs his nose at what makes us a civilized society."

His words had a sing-song quality to them and she relaxed. There was nothing to fear from a man like him.

Then he started moving his fingers toward her pussy and the world became clear and sharp again.

"There must be times when you hate kissing the ass of whoever you're working for," he continued. "They're demanding or indecisive. Maybe they ask for the impossible, or try to stiff you, but you take it because, otherwise, you can't pay your bills."

Maybe he expected her to respond. Maybe he was trying to distract her from his fingers' relentless march. It didn't matter, because not only couldn't she think what to say, she was shivering from the wanting.

"Go back to this morning," he said. A finger grazed her clit. "What happened when you woke up? Did you crawl out of bed and head for the bathroom, or did your hand slip between your legs so you could do this?"

He again touched her clit, the pressure more than the first time and lasting longer. Heat flowed outward from where he'd claimed her.

"I think you played with yourself as long as your bladder allowed. Maybe you didn't sleep well for thinking about what was going to happen."

He was right. She'd spent most of the night wishing morning would come. She'd finally dozed off, only to wake a half hour later with her hands between her legs — much as was happening now.

He released her hair, reached around her and clamped onto her shoulder. "I didn't sleep. The need is stronger than I am."

What need? Besides, was anything stronger than he was?

Certainly not her. She hadn't resisted when he'd pulled her against his chest with her breasts trapped under his arm. A soft sigh escaped her, a sound he surely heard.

"How do you think this going to play out? A few gentle slaps, the hint of a whip followed by sex?"

"Yes." Given his tone, agreeing seemed the easiest course. She was somewhere between lethargic and feeling separated from her body. It belonged to a mindless woman trapped in a big, dark spider's web. Sensual strands stroked the woman and stripped away the last few brain cells.

He went after her, sometimes abrading her flesh, sometimes barely whispering to it. A finger slid into her drenched opening, explored it then exited. She sank down a little, but he hauled her up.

"My way," he said into her ear. "Not yours. In all ways."

Shaking, she waited him out. After what felt like forever, he parted her lips and he entered her again.

"Don't the hell move, understand?"

She nodded.

He took his finger deeper this time, pushing against her pelvic bone so it took all she had not to rise onto her toes. Her pussy muscles tightened around the invasion.

"No!" He squeezed her shoulder. "Damn it, don't move."

Not even that? Confused, because surely he didn't want to deny himself, she fought her body's instinct while he repeatedly plundered and withdrew. Her breathing snagged then escaped in a long hiss.

"Bad slave." He pulled out and slapped her belly. Fire danced there. "I hope to hell you don't expect to be rewarded. You haven't deserved it." He slapped her again, only this time the blow struck her pussy. "Get those damn legs apart."

Yes, Master, yes, Master.

She hoped he'd acknowledge her desire to please him once she'd spread her legs so wide her inner thighs protested. Instead, he clamped hold of her labia. She couldn't breathe.

"This is what happens to slaves who don't obey, got it?"

Did he expect a response? Maybe this was a trick on his part, a test to see how compliant she was. One thing—maybe the only thing—she knew, she loved the sensation.

Loved the fear and anticipation.

"Interested in another chance?"

The foolish creature she'd become nodded.

As he fingered her loose lips, she knew without a doubt that he was deliberately avoiding her clit. So much need was packing inside her, so much emptiness being exposed.

Empty? Had the emotional holes always been there?

"You don't give a damn what it's like for me," he said. He wiped sticky fingers on the inside of her left thigh. "As long as you're getting it, that's the only thing that matters."

"That's not right," she blurted. "I do—"

"I'm not interested." He ground his knuckles where he'd just deposited her juices. "I've dealt with too damn many women like you. I know what they're really like."

You don't know me, she wanted to protest, but that would only set him off more. It hadn't occurred to her that the man playing Dominant to her submission would want more than a hefty paycheck and pleasure. Obviously, she'd been hooked up with someone with a chip on his shoulder.

She had to try to understand him, but how could she if he kept arousing her?

"Not what you expected. Maybe I should have…"

When he didn't continue, she tried to fill in the spaces, but she knew less about him than he did about her. Whoever was behind MSDB, they hadn't adequately screened the men chosen to fulfill the fantasies of women like her, she told herself, only to reconsider because the women she'd seen in the videos had obviously been having wonderful times.

She'd gotten a failure, had she, a sadist?

Fear warred with the need to experience more than the taste of Domination and sex he'd given her. She tugged on her bonds.

"You aren't going anywhere."

Maybe she was reading something that wasn't there into his tone, but he didn't sound as angry as he'd just been. She'd keep her emotional antenna on full alert so she could sense his moods. When the time was right, she'd say whatever he needed to hear. The session might have to be aborted, but at least she'd get out of it intact.

Unless the last few minutes had been an act on his part.

Was that it? He was the consummate actor, a pro who pulled a Dominant cape so firmly around himself that she'd been fooled?

That was it.

All she had to do was play her part.

Simple enough.

"Done talking to yourself?" he asked. "Think you have me figured out?"

She shrugged.

"You don't."

"I want to," she whispered.

Chapter Ten

Things weren't going the way he'd told himself they would. Damn it, the *thing* that had been trying to take hold of him wasn't supposed to win. He was stronger than it. Returning to the island was supposed to have been a test — of something.

Teeth grinding, he had shaken off the woman's soft admission and concentrated on what he'd come here to accomplish today. In the beginning, working for MSDB had been a heady experience. Since he couldn't fight it, by God he'd recapture the sense of power.

Starting with giving the client what she'd paid for and what, for the first year or two, had given his life a depth of satisfaction and meaning his career couldn't.

How much had he told her about his life beyond here?

"I'll forgive you that outburst," he said, determined to take control, "but you'll be punished if you break the rules again. Don't move and don't speak until I say you can."

He didn't bother asking if she understood. There was no hope for her if she didn't get it. Life was too short to spend it trying to educate the uneducable. When, except for the rise and fall of her chest, she remained immobile, he locked onto her. This was about her, not him, and certainly not about the growing storm.

The woman — her name was Shana something — wasn't the most beautiful he'd ever played with, but she might've been the most athletic. Her breasts under his arm carried her heartbeat. He felt the same pulsing life in her pussy. Eager to experience that again, he rolled two fingers over her drenched lips and pushed both into her. She shuddered.

Her knees buckled.

"Straighten yourself, slave. Give your Master full access."

She sucked in more air and straightened. Her head fell back, but the moment it touched his shoulder, she lifted it off him. He understood her desire to keep some part of her separate from him and yet he needed her full surrender.

Needed to own her.

The weight of what he'd just acknowledged pressed on him from all sides. Looking at the window didn't help, because it had started to rain, with the wind beating the trees just as he wanted to beat his slave.

Don't!

Don't let the beast win.

Shana was suspended on the man's fingers. She could fight his hold, but she couldn't win. No matter how hard she struggled, he'd keep her like this for as long as he wanted. The room was darker than it had been earlier, doubtless a result of the impending storm. Shadows seemed to be pressing in on her from all sides, but she wouldn't feel this way if her arms were free and Master's fingers weren't inside her.

Weren't moving, pressing against her channel's sides.

Don't fight. Let it happen.

Everything about how he held her transmitted a single message. He was in control.

Once again, she slipped into a space created by the belief that this moment was part of some grand adventure. She'd wondered what being a submissive woman was like and now she was being given the opportunity to experience it on the deepest levels.

Most importantly, Master's fingers had filled her and were now on the move. The pumping action started slowly but accelerated until she felt awash in sensation. The burning claimed every inch. A small part of her declared that a stranger had no right to manhandle her, but the voice was nearly drowned out by weeks of sexual frustration.

Her fantasy Master had kept her hungry for a long time. She accepted this as wet friction drove her to a steep, familiar edge. He'd often teased her during the weeks he'd kept her in a cage no larger than her closet, commanding her to masturbate while he lightly whipped her thighs, buttocks and back. Not once had he allowed her to come. When she'd been so close to the edge that she'd begged for release, he'd slapped her and ordered her to orally please him. He'd commanded her to swallow as much of his cum as possible and paint her breasts with what she couldn't. Of course she'd obeyed.

Done with her, he'd cuffed her hands behind her so she couldn't get off and left her in the dark.

"Come back to me, damn it!" The man who'd removed her clothes slapped her breasts. "Where the hell did you go?"

She was supposed to answer, to fight the power of the fingers pummeling her.

"My imagination," she got out. "I didn't —"

"What were you imagining?" He pumped her more forcefully, repeatedly slapping her breasts as he did.

"That — that I was your slave and you were denying me." Her pussy muscles clamped down. "Please, oh please."

"Are you begging your Master, slave?"

"Yes." The burning made anything except the truth unthinkable.

"What are you begging him to do?"

Think. Give him what he demands. "To let me climax."

His harsh laugh slapped her senses. "No." He rammed his fingers deep inside her. Bleating like a trapped sheep, she waited for his next move. "Not yet, slave."

* * * *

After his declaration, Master had shoved her away and onto her knees. Half-crazed with need, she'd watched his every move as he walked over to the window and stared out. Even though she couldn't see his expression, his clenched fists and rigid stance said he was struggling with something. An occasional flash of light served as testament to the lightning accompanying the storm. Thunder roared. After several minutes he turned around. His eyes had shifted from gray to black. There was something fierce about him, a wild, savage quality that spoke to every inch of her.

"Crawl over to me," he commanded.

She felt awkward and ungainly obeying, so aware of their bodies she could hardly stand it. The top and bra that had once stood as defense against his power now imprisoned her when she longed to be free of all clothing.

"Good," he said when she was a few inches from him. "You have promise."

"Thank you, Master."

He took hold of the hair at the top of her head. "You think of me as your Master?"

"I don't know."

"Do you want to take that step?"

"I don't know."

"What if you had no choice?"

Unease had her testing her restraints. "Is that a threat?"

"Or a promise."

She was still trying to make sense of what he'd said when he closed his hands over her arms and hauled her to her feet. He spun her away from him. "Don't move."

Judging by the sounds he was making, he'd gone to the storage box in the living room and was taking something out of it. From where she was, she couldn't see the bed where he'd placed the vibrator. Standing there with nothing to do but anticipate increased her awareness of the burning in her shoulders. As long as she didn't fight the rope it didn't dig into her wrists, but they were sensitive. From what she understood of the BDSM lifestyle, the inflicting and acceptance of pain was a core component of a Dominant/submissive relationship. She'd watched open-mouthed and turned on as MSDB operatives lashed restrained women who obviously loved what was being done to them.

When would her time come and how would she handle it?

"Don't move, got it?"

The command lifted her head.

"Got it?" he repeated. "I'm about to take you even deeper. Whether you comply or resist makes no difference, but it'll go easier for you if you do as you're ordered. This is the only chance you'll have to get with the program. One way or the other, it's going to happen."

The unknown fueled her anticipation.

"Are you deliberately keeping quiet?" His hand landed on her shoulder. "Checking to see what angers me?"

"No. I didn't mean —"

"Doesn't matter. In fact, not much about you as a separate human being matters to me because that isn't going to last long."

She cursed his attempts to fuck with her mind. At the same time, his heavy hand served as an inescapable reminder of who was in charge.

"You're an object, a piece of clay in need of molding. Whether you see yourself as perfect or destroyed by the time I've finished with you depends on many things." He ran his fingers into her hair at the nape of her neck. "You can ponder what you want from the process or simply let it happen. That doesn't concern me. Only the end product does."

The thought that he might be losing his hold on his boundaries set her heart pounding and yet, in some respects, he was right. She was clay, unmolded, desperate to see the end result.

"This is proof of your subservience," he said as he slipped something around her neck and fastened it in place. Metal settled over her flesh. "You may have thought I had to ask permission before collaring you, but that's not how it's going to be."

By moving her head about, she determined that the collar was more than an inch wide. It didn't restrict her breathing and wasn't particularly heavy, not that she could dismiss its presence, which she had no doubt had been his intention. Looking down, she glimpsed a ring dangling from the collar. She wouldn't have been surprised if there was another ring in back, perfect for attaching chains or rope to.

Enslaved. Brought to her knees. Drawn into another world.

"I wondered..." she managed, before running out of thought.

"What? Whether we'd get to this? It was never in doubt."

He came around her, trailing his fingers over her hips as he did and positioned himself so the window was behind him. She still caught glimpses of the storm-trapped trees, and the sound of the rain striking the glass was like drumming. Because she'd worked through countless Florida storms, she knew how hot and close the air out there was, how hard breathing could become.

"I have a test for you," he said. "How you perform won't change anything for me, but I'm curious to see how deep you are into what's happening. Call it a measure of acceptance — or resistance, depending on your actions."

She licked her lips. "Do you want me to say anything?"

The corners of his mouth lifted. "Not long ago it would have never occurred to you that you should ask that question. Most times I prefer silence, but it might amuse me to hear your observations."

He hooked a forefinger through the collar ring and lifted it, making her arch her spine. "I'm going to untie your wrists, but there's no reason for you to assume you're anywhere near free. I simply want to give you the opportunity to participate more fully in your submission."

She tried to nod — no easy task, considering he still had a firm hold on the ring. Arousal worked through her in waves, keeping her so off balance she could barely concentrate. One second she fought an almost desperate desire to run for safety, the next she longed to plunge fully into her new reality.

"Submission," he repeated. "How does the word make you feel?"

"Nervous. Anticipating."

"And that surprises you."

"Yes," she answered the non-question. "At least I, ah, guess it does. I wasn't sure how I'd respond here."

"No first-timer does." The pressure on her neck eased until she no longer had to look at the ceiling. He still had hold of the ring and could easily reinforce his message of power. "Then, although you might find this hard to believe, eventually the thrill goes out of the game. What was once new and exciting becomes ordinary — unless..."

Maybe she should have been accustomed to how he seemed to lose his train of thought, but she couldn't help wondering if it was a matter of him deliberately stopping himself from saying too much. Her family had always been straight shooters. They spoke their minds. A man who did the opposite confused and alarmed her.

But then she'd said damn little about what had brought her here.

"Let me see your hands," he commanded and drew his finger out of the ring.

His nails left pinpricks of heat on her throat as she swiveled away from him. Teeth clenched, she presented him with her back. She wasn't close to being comfortable with having her ass exposed, but awareness of how much he could see of her came in second to anticipating what he would do next.

"Don't expect me to do all the work." He lifted her hands off her buttocks. "Stay just like that."

Keeping her arms elevated made her shoulders burn, but for reasons she only partly comprehended, she wanted to please him — if that were possible. When he was done untying the ropes around her wrists, he positioned her arms by her sides and reached around her. He looped the rope through the collar ring, leaving the ends to hang between her breasts. Then he again spun her toward him once more and laced his fingers through hers. She felt connected to him, the other half of something larger than them.

"Squeeze. I need to see whether you've lost strength."

Barely caring, she complied. Not long ago she'd looked into his eyes and should have remembered everything about them, but there was nothing familiar about the black orbs. His nearness enveloped her, marched her toward the cave where he lived.

"I'm not afraid," she whispered.

"You should be." He lifted her right arm and started wrapping the rope around her wrist.

Hyper aware of the flames trapped under the strands, she recorded his every move. When he'd finished, he seized her other arm and repeated the task. Both arms were now deeply bent with her fingers under her chin and her hands once more useless.

He pushed her back, folded his arms across his considerable chest and studied what he'd accomplished. "You're so easy. There's no fight to you."

"Is that what you want, me struggling?"

"Maybe."

Beneath the 'maybe' she heard *yes*. Her mind slipped back into the world of make-believe. She was a member of a rebel group determined to overthrow the ruling party, and her task had been to use sex to distract the guards. But she'd been found out, tied up and brought before the military leader. Instead of killing her, he'd declared she was more useful alive. He'd promised his men they could have her once he was done with her then dismissed the troops.

Now it was just the two of them. She was his prisoner.

Chapter Eleven

"You shouldn't have come here," her captor said. Like earlier, his words brought her back to reality. "You might regret it."

Wondering if he'd tapped into her fantasy, she said the only thing she could think of. "I can't leave. If I do, I'll deal with the consequences."

"Yeah." He seized her elbows and lifted them. "You will."

Suddenly he was propelling her backward across the room. He slammed her into a wall so hard she was stunned. "Too late. Too damn late."

Don't say anything to set him off. See if you can bring him back.

"I'm not just a Dom," he told her. "Sometimes, I become a predator. This is one of those times. A predator takes what he wants and I want you."

Thoughts of pacifying him evaporated, leaving her full of his words and strength. She curled her useless fingers tightly and fixed her gaze at the man who now put her in mind of a wolf.

"Naked."

He gave no indication of what he had in mind when he turned his back on her and walked out of the room. She stared at the open doorway with her senses straining, trying to determine what he was doing. She thought about leaving the wall but didn't take the chance.

Naked, he'd said and naked he'd do.

When he returned, the scissors he'd used on her earlier dangled from fingers that dwarfed the tool. The way he was regarding her, she wasn't sure he was aware of what he held.

"You should have run. Shouldn't have let me capture you," he said.

"I couldn't help it. You were faster and stronger, well armed." She couldn't say whether she was playing along in an attempt to placate him or had become a willing participant in this rainy day's scene.

"And I'm experienced in not letting the enemy escape."

She'd become the enemy in his mind? Something about seeing him as an opposing force kicked her libido up a notch. This wasn't a stand-off between equals. They'd been at war until he'd rendered her helpless. Now she was his.

Belonged to him.

She gnawed on her lower lip. "What are you going to do with me?" she finally thought to ask. "Maybe hold me for ransom?"

"I'm not sure you're worth anything to your tribe."

A tribe? Where had he gone mentally? "I'm the chief's daughter and a warrior in my own right. Of course I'm valuable."

His chuckle held no warmth. "A true warrior wouldn't have let herself be caught so easily. It's time for you to learn what happens to those I don't see as my equal—those I've enslaved."

Concerned the *game* might have taken a dangerous turn, she pressed herself against the wall. If he tried anything—anything he hadn't already, that is—she'd knee him where a man hated being kneed. Hopefully, that would bring him to his senses.

"I don't want to be your slave. Untie me."

"No."

"Why not? Are you afraid I might do the same to you?"

"That'll never happen." He extended the scissors toward her.

Driven by self-preservation, she lowered her head and charged. She slammed into his chest, rattling her mind.

"I don't like this!" Fighting to stay conscious, she continued to push at him.

He took a backward step then planted his feet against her middle, easily shoving her to the wall. She fought the ropes rendering her arms useless as fiercely as she did his greater strength.

"The prisoner believes she can escape. Time to teach her how wrong she is."

She didn't recognize his voice. Caution argued with instinct, telling her to give up and go along with whatever his plan was, but maybe he hadn't planned any of this.

Maybe he'd changed more than his voice had.

"You can't do this!" She tried to kick him, but he easily swept her foot aside. "You have no right."

If he heard her argument, he gave no indication. After letting her struggle to free herself from his all-possessive hand and the damned wall until her muscles trembled, he grabbed both wrist ropes in one hand and hauled her over to the bed. He half-lifted her and threw her face down onto it.

"I like a fighter. Makes it all worthwhile."

Wondering what he meant distracted her from everything except making sure she could breathe.

"I've drawn this out long enough," he said. "Deprived myself too long."

He was going to rape her, turn what had started out so exciting into something awful. She grew weak at the understanding that begging him not to continue on this path wouldn't change anything. Not sure what she had in mind, she tried to lift her upper body.

"No, slave." He planted his hand on the space between her shoulder blades and pushed her back down. "Not until it's what I want."

This was all wrong, an abomination, the start of a nightmare.

She was still trying to wrap her mind around that when he took hold of her T-shirt's hem and pulled it away from her waist. A snipping sound, along with the loss of tension against her breasts, left no doubt that he was cutting the garment off her. He pulled the two halves from her back. As long as she remained on her belly, her breasts were safe. He severed her bra along her spine and at the straps.

"Get it." He slapped her buttocks. "Message delivered."

"I get it," she retorted through clenched teeth.

Her words filled her with resolve not to become a blubbering mess. Besides—and who knew whether he was aware of it—the most recent manhandling had gotten her juices flowing again. She really was a slut, a submission-loving slut.

As long as it didn't go too far.

He dropped the scissors onto the floor and grabbed her destroyed bra. He pulled it off her and placed it near her body.

"The woman warrior should have come dressed for battle. You've made it too easy for me."

"Would it have made any difference? Now that you've captured me, you can do whatever you want."

When he didn't agree with or deny her comment, she decided to continue to play into his delusion. "Who are you? Maybe a war lord? Do you have any code of honor or do you believe all spoils belong to the victor?"

A strong, broad hand rested on the base of her spine. "You belong to me. That's all you need to know."

As if that wasn't enough.

Her arms couldn't have been any more useless, and she knew better than to try to get off the bed—a bed that was supposed to play a major role in the MSDB experience. Maybe to give herself something to focus on so she wouldn't go mad, she thought back to when she'd naively believed she'd wind up having consensual sex with her Dominant. She'd grown wet thinking about how he'd guide her into submission, imagined herself kneeling at his feet with her lips around his erection while staring adoringly up at him. He might slap her face a few times or place a strip of leather around her neck. They'd call each other 'Master' and 'slave' while trying not to laugh at the words of pretend.

This was no pretend. He wouldn't have destroyed her clothes if it had been.

"You'll never stop dreaming of getting free," he said from where he loomed over her. "No matter what your captor does to you, your spirit won't let go of that faint possibility. Thoughts of freedom will keep you alive. They'll also give me what I want to play off."

When she'd first landed on the bed, her legs had been apart. She'd brought them as close together as she dared without drawing attention to what she was doing and had forgotten about her lower body. Awareness of that part of her returned in a rush as he eased his hand between her ass cheeks.

"What are you — ?"

"Nervous, slave? You should be."

Was she a slave or a captive? Maybe it didn't matter.

"You came here full of yourself. You thought everything would be designed for your pleasure. Unfortunately, you failed to take me into consideration."

"I didn't," she insisted as something, his thumb maybe, pressed against her anus. "I — oh please — I assumed you'd get off by — "

"But it didn't really matter." The pressure increased. "You put yourself first. The bitches always do."

If that was how he saw the women who paid for what MSDB offered, why was he working for the organization? She couldn't imagine being associated with a group that had no consideration for —

"Nowhere for you to go, is there, slave?" He punctuated his question by barely slipping his thumb into her back end. Thank goodness he'd coated his digit with her juices before forcing the semi-invasion. "Out of options."

She'd never consented to anal sex because she hadn't found a man she trusted to take her like that. Master was right. She had no options, nothing she could do except lie there while he explored her. She couldn't stop tensing or trying to pull her hands free. At the same time, having that part of her invaded by this man sent her to a place defined by hues of red and black.

His thumb advanced and retreated, plundered and withdrew, each time taking her deeper into the journey. It hurt and yet it didn't. Against all reason, she bent her knees and lifted her lower body off the bed.

"Down into my cave." He blew a hot breath over her spine. "Down to a place of darkness and longing."

Longing. The word expanded and became reality. Much as she hated herself for giving in so easily, she had no choice. His thumb continued to plug her rear opening. At the same time, the fingers of his other hand were on the move, slipping ever closer to her pussy.

Somewhere, the warriors of her clan were talking about what might have happened to the woman who'd fought beside them. They wouldn't believe it if they could see her now, might have believed a witch or evil shaman had cast a spell over her to turn her into this wanton, helpless slut.

"Not ashamed of yourself?" He flicked a finger over her clit. "You should be."

Heat roared through her and threatened to throw her into the flames he'd created. Suddenly scared, she dropped back down on the bed.

"Don't. Oh please, don't."

"Too late, slave. You're mine."

Chapter Twelve

Shana tried to separate her legs, only to stop when the ropes now around her ankles dug into them. After demonstrating his power over her rear opening, the man who'd called her slave had left her to open the small window. Energy from the warm, electricity-filled storm circled the room and pressed against her skin. Now that he'd finished changing her restraints, he stood staring at her. She knew what lust looked like in a man's eyes, but his expression went beyond that. There were added layers and a glimpse of something inhuman.

Despite that, she wasn't afraid. She should've been. After all, she'd never been more helpless or alone.

No, not alone, because Master stood over her holding the vibrator he'd presented at the beginning of whatever this was. After tethering her ankles with soft cotton rope, he'd again tied her hands behind her. The whole time he'd worked on her, she'd lain there trembling and excited. Probably out of her mind.

Neither of them had spoken.

He extended his hand and rested the vibrator between her breasts. Her shaking increased.

"My clan attacked yours," he said. "A few died, others were wounded. When your chief knew his people had lost, he agreed to talk to my clan's leaders about putting an end to the hostilities."

Play into his fantasy, if that's what it is. "What were they fighting about?"

"Land. Access to water."

That made as much sense as anything in this crazy

scenario. "My people had staked a claim to that land and refused to let yours use the water? Why wouldn't they share?"

He raked his free hand through his hair and moved his gaze from her breasts to her eyes and back to her breasts.

"They insisted the lake was sacred, a gift to them from the spirits," he said.

"Oh." What was she supposed to say, that she understood? She didn't and yet his explanation was as logical as anything else given — given what?

"Your chief didn't want to anger the spirits by allowing unbelievers to spoil the water, but he no longer had a choice. He didn't want any more warriors to die so he agreed to listen to the terms of peace. My chief made demands. They included you."

"Me?" The vibrator was now the same temperature as her body. She could almost dismiss its presence. Almost.

"You're the chief's daughter. My clan's leaders know they'll be safe as long as you're with them. Your father had no choice but to turn you over to us. You became our prisoner."

"Where are the rest of your people?" Maybe logic would get through to him. She at least had to try. "Where did they take me?"

He shook his head and briefly closed his eyes. When he opened them, nothing had changed. The flickering, inhuman quality was still there.

"My chief turned you over to me so I could prepare you to receive the other warriors."

Receive? Hardly. Just the same, she knew not to press him about the word's true meaning.

"What...?" She swallowed. "What are you going to do to prepare me?"

Now that the window was open, she clearly heard the wind attacking the trees. Rain hammered at the building. Some of that moisture ran down the inner wall beneath the window, making it more difficult for her to find the line between this room and the wilderness. If the storm continued, it might consume her.

"I will do many things," he muttered.

Before she could ask for clarification, even before she could decide whether that was wise, he leaned over her, flattened her right breast with his free hand and settled her onto her back. Her weight rested on her arms. She again tried moving her legs.

"Pleasure and pain. Taking you on a journey that'll change you. Introduce you to what your body is capable of and make you a slave to it."

What she'd learned about BDSM had led her to conclude that was the practice's deepest appeal. Women who embraced being submissive loved surrendering their bodies to the incomprehensible, to her, mix of sexual pleasure and physical punishment. She wondered if, now that he'd justified his reasons for having her under his control, he'd dismissed the notion that they were members of warring clans or tribes. From now on he'd simply wear his Master hat and expect her to embrace her own role — one he'd taken out of her hands.

With her approval.

"The human body is amazing," he said. "Much of the time it does its job without our having to direct it. We breathe without thinking, don't have to remind our hearts to beat. Our skin alerts us to changes in temperature so we can put on or remove clothing." He lifted the vibrator off her and turned it on, then held it up so she could see the vibrations. "A person accepts a gentle touch and recoils from danger. We seldom give our bodies the credit they're due." He frowned. "Sometimes we have no choice but to give that remarkable system our full attention."

Watching her like a hawk watches a mouse, he slowly brought the vibrator to within an inch of the nipple he hadn't buried under his hand. She held her breath.

"Even before contact is made, your system sends a message to your brain that something important is about to happen."

She might've argued that her brain and not her nerve endings had stopped her breathing. Any second, any damned second he'd —

"Your silence interests me." He nodded in what might've been approval. "Maybe you're waiting for permission, but I don't think so. It's too early in your education."

Education?

The rapidly moving tool brushed her nipple. The contact lasted less than a second, not enough time for her nerves to do more than jump.

"I enjoy this part." He rested the vibrator against the inside of her breast. "Keeping a slave off balance and demonstrating my power. My ability to both pleasure and pester her."

She didn't care what he called what he was doing, because the movement spiraling throughout her breast felt so damn good. Her awareness of her compromised limbs retreated. The sensation had already reached her belly and was heading south.

"What is this?" he asked. "Good or bad?"

"Good." What would she gain by lying, except to, maybe, anger him?

"Correct."

This wasn't some test question she'd answered to his satisfaction. She'd stay where he wanted her to be, respond as best she could, live with this music humming through her.

He moved the vibrator in a slow circle around her breast, and when he was done, he made another circuit, this one closer to her nipple. She ducked her head so she could watch. Her toes curled and her nails dug into her palms. Moisture dampened her core.

"Still good?"

"Yes. Oh yes."

Watching her, he rested the vibrator on her nipple. "Yes what?"

"Master." Her throat felt dry.

"Don't forget that."

As distracting as the touch was, she noted his warning tone. She didn't dare relax after all, because things might change in a heartbeat and she needed to be prepared.

Prepared for what? she wondered as the pressure increased. *Sudden pain?*

"You might believe you understand what this is about, but you're a baby, a novice, a virgin."

That, she wasn't.

"Time for kindergarten."

When the vibrator's contact with her nipple remained constant, she relaxed a little. He'd stopped studying her expression and had turned his attention back to her breasts. She continued to watch for a change in his eyes. The fast-paced movement on her nipple was arousing, but not like what she experienced when she used one on her sex.

He'd lifted his hand off the breast he'd been covering before she noticed what he'd done. He brought it close to her face then placed it behind his back. "Think about this for a moment. What does your Master intend to do next?"

She didn't know and could only imagine. Her imaginings took her from anticipation to dread then to confusion as the vibrator continued its insistent attack. She hated her helplessness but loved how he'd used it to bring her pleasure—so far.

He snapped his fingers, forcing her to acknowledge the empty hand hovering over her. She stared at the closely trimmed nails, prominent knuckles and broad palm.

"Ever wear nipple clamps?" He closed his thumb and forefinger over her nipple, the grip strong.

"No. No, Master." She sucked in her belly.

"Ever want one?"

"I, ah, I've thought about it but I don't really—I don't think so, Master."

"But if that's what your Master wants, you don't have a choice." He tightened his hold.

For the first time, true discomfort slapped at her senses. Afraid to move, she held her breath. Damp air lay heavily against her naked body. The building shuddered from a powerful blast of wind.

"Pay attention. Note the conflicting sensations on your breasts. One" — he started the vibrator in a tight circle around her rock-hard nipple — "is sexual while the other isn't."

"I..."

"What were you going to say, slave?"

That you're scaring me. But that would've been an admission of failure and defeat when she prided herself on never giving up. "Nothing, Master."

"I don't believe you."

He's going to hurt me.

Chapter Thirteen

Only it wasn't that simple, she admitted, as he continued tormenting one nipple while treating the other to the opposite. Maybe her system had made a deliberate decision to throw as much focus as possible on the hot pinpricks of pleasure carving a path from where the vibrator was working to her pussy.

Her trapped nipple burned and ached. Despite her attempts not to, she couldn't help trying to break free. Thrashing helped distract her from the conflicting sensations. It wasn't enough, of course. She still stood perched between desire and dread, but as long as she kept moving she wouldn't drown.

Maybe.

"This is more than kindergarten." He drew her nipple up and down, left and right. "You've in grade school now. Maybe you're looking forward to mid high."

"No."

"No, what?" He turned off the vibrator and placed it on the bed near her leg.

"Master. Master."

"Too late."

"I'm sorry, Master. I didn't mean..." Much as she hated her pleading tone, her breast was on fire. She struggled to wrench away from him, only to sob and roll back when he seized her other breast and clamped down on it.

"There are Doms and then there are Doms. I'm the bastard kind." He equalized the pressure on her breasts until it felt as if her entire upper body were under attack. "I tried the conventional route, the game playing MSDB is known for, but that isn't me. It used to be, but..."

Despite the battering her nerves were under, she noted that his voice had dropped at the end. She fought to rise above the pain and concentrate on him.

"Do you miss what you used to be, Master? Maybe you don't understand who you've become."

He'd left her on the bed so he could go to the window, where the air his lungs craved was, but now that he was there he felt even less in control than when he'd first opened the window.

He needed to gag her again. Hell, he should have already silenced her.

Why? Are you afraid of what she asked you?

The hell I am, he told himself, but maybe it was a lie. Otherwise, he would have shrugged off her comment about him not understanding who he'd become.

Rain blasted through the screen and struck him in the face. Water dripped off the end of his nose and ran down his cheeks. He wasn't sure when it had started raining. Maybe the downpour had been going on for days.

The storm had him in its grip, the hold stronger here on the island than if he'd been on the mainland. For the past few years, he'd been debating whether he should move to a less humid area, and not just because he hated being hot and sticky all summer. But his job, house and friends were here.

So was MSDB and the opportunity to indulge his Dominant urges.

The problem, he admitted as his vision cleared enough so he could see his slave-in-training, was that they were more than urges. 'Inescapable' was more like it.

He wanted and needed to dominate women. Controlling their actions and reactions completed him. Molding their thoughts and how they saw him turned him on.

As he made his way back to the bed, he acknowledged that, in today's world, he couldn't really own a woman, a slave, but if she wanted it—

"Your breasts are red," he told her unnecessarily. "Hard to tell which received what treatment."

Her eyes were so damned big, the pupils huge and staring. She was shaking but not, he knew, in terror. He ran his hand between her legs. Wet heat greeted him. Pleased, he licked his fingers. She watched his every move.

He again ran his fingers over her sex, taking his time. When he'd gathered some of her juices, he placed his fingers against her mouth. She sucked. "Does that surprise you? Maybe you didn't think you'd react like that to pain."

"I didn't know, Master."

He didn't want to kiss her, damn it, didn't want to connect with her that way. But then the storm sighed. He needed to share something with the woman he'd pulled into his demented world. Maybe she craved the same thing because, instead of averting her face, she lifted her head what little she could and met him halfway. He took hold of her shoulders and supported her, brought her even closer to him. Her mouth parted. He felt warmth and wetness. Her trembling slipped into him and made him vulnerable. Despite the threat, he extended his tongue. She pushed back, said something about equality despite an unequal day. He dove and retreated until the force that owned him demanded he take over.

Growling deep in his throat, he pushed her against the bed, sucked her lower lip between his teeth and nibbled. She squirmed but kept her head still. Her answering growl was higher pitched but just as honest.

She wanted him. Damn wanted him.

Shaken by the thought, he released her and straightened while still holding her down. She looked so deliciously helpless with her eyes glimmering and mouth sagging.

His.

To command.

"I'm in charge, get it?" He punctuated his comment by slapping her cheek. "Don't you for a second think otherwise."

She nodded, but beneath her shock, he saw something else, a wisdom that hadn't been there before.

This woman knew where he was wounded.

Master's wet hair clung to his head. Droplets stuck to his eyebrows. One drew her attention to the lashes of his right eye. Her cheek still stung from where he'd slapped her, but despite the pain she understood. For a moment, they'd come closer than he'd expected or felt comfortable with, and he was trying to eradicate the message behind the kiss.

He might not let them return to when everything had been about getting to know each other, but he couldn't take away the memory. The feel of his lips on hers and their tongues dancing would stay with her forever.

"I have to go to the bathroom," she said. "I need you to — Master, I don't want to..."

"You're asking permission to use the toilet?"

Permission. Yes, that was one of the things that defined their relationship. She nodded and flexed her right knee a little. She wasn't sure she could get off the bed without help and shouldn't try until he gave permission. She'd been unaware of her bladder until suddenly its demand overrode everything else.

"Damn," he said. "I should have — all right." He slipped a forefinger through the ring at the front of her collar and pulled up.

Feeling her helplessness throughout, she strained to bring her body upright. When she was sitting, he released the ring, clamped hold of her hips and slid her to the edge of the bed so her legs dangled over it.

She stood without help but nearly fell when she tried to take a step. Another wave of helplessness distracted her from her bladder.

"I'm not your servant," he snapped. "Figure it out."

She started scooting her feet over the floor. Her breasts jiggled and the collar ring bobbed. She had to lean over a little to keep from losing her balance, wondering all the while what was going to happen once she reached the closed door. Either he opened it or risked her peeing standing in front of it. Even though she hated appearing so awkward, the situation kept her sexually on alert. Maybe it was because everything that was happening revolved around her.

Master walked beside her with his attention locked on her naked and restrained body. Nothing else mattered to him.

Maybe.

To her relief, he opened the door, revealing a pristine and spacious bathroom with both a shower and jetted tub. She hadn't had a tub bath since childhood. This one was large enough to hold two people.

Closing down the thought, she acknowledged that Master intended to watch while she performed what should've been a private act.

Not looking at him, she sat on the toilet. Even though it probably made no difference to him, she took small pride in slowly letting go. Thanks to the rain, the sound of her urine hitting the water in the bowl was muffled. Done, she repeatedly clenched her muscles down there while bouncing up and down a little.

"You think that's good enough?" he demanded. "It isn't."

She made herself face him. She couldn't read his expression, had no idea what he was thinking.

"What do you want me to do, Master?"

"Lean forward." He reached for the toilet paper.

Her throat tight, she did as he'd commanded. Desperate to not have to think about what he was doing, she pictured herself jogging down the path leading from the cabin to where the boat that would take her back home waited. In her mind, it had stopped raining and steam rose from the saturated ground to coat her naked body.

"Back to the bed," he said after he'd washed his hands. "Time for more lessons."

The intoxicating scent of a summer storm filled her senses

as she shuffled into the bedroom. The coverlet was wrinkled, the vibrator on the floor. He stepped back and watched as she wriggled and scooted until her ass was securely on the bed and her legs over the side. He folded his arms over his still-clothed chest and ran his gaze from her tangled hair to her toes digging into the carpet. Noting his tight jaw and the hard mound beneath his zipper, she struggled to retain her emotional equilibrium. If only she'd known how much the *encounter* would do to her mind.

"What now?" she snapped. "More of the damned same?"

Even when his lips thinned, she didn't regret her outburst. This might've been a game to him — might — but for her, everything was at stake.

"That's how you see what's happened so far?" he asked. "It's something to be tolerated?"

"I didn't say — no, not 'tolerated'. Master."

When the corner of his mouth twitched, she felt the movement in the pit of her stomach.

"What, then?"

Hadn't he already asked her something like this? If he had, how had she responded? Hoping she could get away with silence, she fixed her attention on her knees, or rather, she tried to. Even though she couldn't see her core, she imagined the pale dusting of hair that didn't completely cover her pussy. The first time she'd used a mirror to study that part of her anatomy, she'd been shocked by how dark and wrinkly things were there, but she'd only been eleven or twelve. Since then, she'd embraced what identified her as a woman, especially her clit.

Hell, she loved what it was capable of.

"I guess I'm ready for whatever, Master."

Her hope that he'd say they were on the same page died when he didn't acknowledge her comment. His intense stare broke her apart a bit, so she didn't know whether anticipation or hesitancy held the upper hand. Bits and pieces of MSDB scenes were messing with her mind, including the ones that showed women wearing nipple clamps while being lashed. Just because their moans had been filled with passion didn't mean she'd react the same way.

Not that he cared.

That, she forced herself to accept as he headed into the living room, had been in his eyes almost from the beginning.

Chapter Fourteen

He could have moved both storage boxes into the bedroom before the sub had showed up, but he hadn't during the hour or so he'd sat in the living room asking himself if he dared stay. Instead of preparing the space in the room where he'd left her for action, he'd stared out of the open door while trying to deny the island's hold on him. Finally, he'd stood, stepped outside and headed down the path toward where Heaven and Hell, in the form of a female body, waited.

The short walk filled him with reverence for the setting but did nothing to clear his mind. Feeling half drunk, he lifted the lid on the well-equipped sex toy box, but instead of finishing the task, he let it slam closed. The sane part of him knew he was risking too much by letting the environment engulf him, but the beast was so strong. As water-heavy air continued to blast him, he sucked in as much of it as his lungs could hold.

Wilderness. Wild. An end to civilization.

Heady with a repeat of what had claimed him more times than he wanted to acknowledge, he gave himself up to nature's strength. His clothes became so wet they felt as if they were glued to him. Fighting the pulsing in his cock, he yanked his shirt over his head and dropped it onto the deck. Wind-driven rain slammed into his bare flesh. He opened his mouth and sucked in liquid. After holding the water in his mouth for several seconds, he slowly swallowed. The storm's essence ran down his throat and entered his belly. He stuck out his tongue.

Nothing had ever felt more right.

Or dangerous.

A half dozen swallows later, he went inside. He could see the slave through the door between the living room and bedroom and wondered what she was thinking and whether she'd deluded herself into believing she understood him. That was impossible, of course.

She never would.

Master was naked from the waist up. Maybe she should try to determine what he was holding, but she couldn't take her gaze from the broad, glistening chest with countless droplets clinging to the dark hair and highlighting his well-defined muscles. She'd never understood who had decided that today's male models should have all their chest hair removed. Someone, somewhere, must have thought a man looked sexier that way and everyone else had followed suit, but they were wrong.

The man striding toward her was pure male.

"You went outside," she said unnecessarily. Why was remaining silent suddenly so hard? "Any sign of the storm letting up?"

He didn't acknowledge her comment. In fact, he barely seemed aware that he wasn't the only one in the room as he placed what he'd chosen for her next lesson near the foot of the bed. Her head buzzing, she noted nipple clamps attached by a silver chain, a thin whip, a ball gag, a blindfold, a butt plug. There were other items, but she couldn't focus on them.

I don't know if I'm going to survive.

"You're so damn sure of yourself," she blurted. "What makes you think I want all this shit?"

His eyes feral, he knocked her sideways onto the bed and lifted her legs so they, too, were on it. She bent her knees so she wouldn't roll one way or the other. Her unruly hair partly obscured her view of him.

"I didn't mean it that way, Master," she blathered. "I'm just nervous. You must have seen my list of the kinds of behavior that are within my comfort zone. No anal sex."

He raked her hair back from her eyes. This was no lover's gesture and she couldn't begin to describe his expression. She'd briefly dated a man who was into boxing and had reluctantly attended a couple of local matches with him. What had caught her attention the most had been the way the young, fierce boxers had acted while they'd waited for a match to start. They were stereotypical pit bulls straining at their leashes, wild horses determined to break out of their corrals.

Master had too much of that in him.

"I want this to be educational and exciting," she told him. "I came here of my own free will and paid good money for—am I getting through to you? Don't spoil it for me. Don't make me regret—"

"I don't give a damn."

She struggled to sit up, but he planted his hand on the side of her neck, where the collar rested.

"I can't believe you don't." She was alive all right, every part of her in overdrive. "If you hurt me, really hurt me, you know I'll tell the authorities. I'll make sure they shut MSDB down."

His only response was to clamp his hand over her mouth. He was so close that his wet heat became part of her. The feral quality had faded from his gaze, replaced by a predator's look. This was no act. He hadn't decided to assume a role in an attempt to add an element to her experience. Maybe she should take his comment that he didn't give a damn about her to heart, but she couldn't.

Or maybe the truth was she couldn't yet let herself go there.

"You think you know your body," he said, "but you haven't touched its depths. Neither have I gone all the way into mine. That's going to change."

If his taut muscles were any indication, he'd had to work at getting the words out. Not for the first time she took note of the two sides of him—the dangerous and the civilized.

He, again, became a conquering warrior in her mind and she his helpless prisoner. He'd been trained to fight and defend and punish those who threatened his clan's safety. It didn't matter to him that she was the enemy chief's daughter and not an enemy warrior. He'd exact his brand of justice on her.

Only it wasn't that simple.

His finger pressed onto her closed mouth while his other hand continued to rest on her neck.

"Captive," he muttered. "Hostage and slave. That's what you are."

His hands seemed to envelop her entire body. He could've easily broken her neck. Even as she told herself he wouldn't do that, she wasn't sure the consequences of killing her had entered his head because he was in a space she hadn't reached.

Yet.

"You think I'm all three things?" she asked around his fingers.

"Yes."

There was that deep and seductive tone again, the one designed to open up her veins and crawl inside her. She stared, wide-eyed, up at her captor.

"Where are we?" she asked.

He lifted his hand from her mouth and ran his thumb from the base of the collar to the valley between her breasts. He teased one breast then the other. His eyes were still those of a predator, but he didn't look quite as hungry as he had a few minutes before. There was no need for him to kill his prey or for the conquering warrior to slash his prisoner's throat and all the time in the world to demonstrate his strength.

"Where?" he repeated. "In the jungle."

"How did we get here?"

He frowned. "Does it matter?"

"I just wanted—"

"You belong to me. That's the only thing you need to

know."

The way his hand was separating her breasts and pressing against her heart, she thought better of asking what had made him come to that decision. What she couldn't wrap her mind around, any more than she could deny the sensation, was how being dominated by him made her feel. She'd been turned on for a long time today. Sometimes, sexual wanting had been a little need humming in the background, but several times it had become everything.

She was again approaching that state.

"You're made for action," he said. "Every part of you screams sex."

"And you like that."

He neither agreed with nor denied her comment, not that she cared, starting at the moment he picked up the vibrator and placed it against her labia. She clamped her legs together as if cradling it. Positioned the way it was, it would stay in place as long as she remained on her side.

"Not fighting, captive?"

His arms hung by his sides, as if testing her will. She had no doubt he wanted to see how long she'd hold out before begging him to turn it on but, although she did in spades, a small, sane part of her commanded her to see if he could keep his hands off her. This man she barely comprehended wanted her. She saw the truth of that in his burning gaze and the way his fingers were extended toward his cock, the occasional shifting of his legs. The same need gnawed at her, a strange, hungry beast that might overcome her at any time.

This wasn't fair! She had no way of testing his limits.

If she wanted to.

"Is that what you want me to do?" Hoping for more stimulation against her sex, she tightened her thigh muscles even more. The strain made them shudder, giving her away. "You get off on watching me struggle?"

"That, and watching you suffer."

His comment sucked all moisture from her throat. As

she understood it, 'suffering' meant different things within the BDSM community. Sometimes, sexual stimulation was incorporated into a punishment session, sometimes not.

"You already got what you wanted when you pinched my nipple."

He laughed, a short harsh sound. "Not even close, slave."

She couldn't stop herself from trying to roll onto her belly when he picked up the nipple clamps. A barely audible, "Please don't," escaped, despite her attempt to keep it inside. Maybe he didn't hear, because he didn't say anything, but perhaps he'd returned to the jungle he'd mentioned earlier.

As he demonstrated how the adjustable screws worked, and the rubber tips, she fought apprehension.

Not just apprehension, she admitted, as moisture began to coat the vibrator. Instead of wanting to get the hell out of there, she shivered in anticipation of having her nipples imprisoned. He took his damned sweet time bringing the clamps to her breasts, and she nearly screamed when he repositioned the breast closest to the bed so he could get to that nipple. When he had it where he wanted it, he cupped his hand around her other breast and squeezed.

"Done," he said and opened the clamp's jaws wide. "Perfect for getting you where I want you."

The rubber-tipped steel closed around the base of her nipple, taking bites of her sanity as it did. She gasped and stretched her neck as if that stupid move would free her.

"Feel your capture. Understand how completely you're under my control."

The clamp tightened down and took a bite. Alarmed and excited, she bent her neck so she could see what he'd done. Silver now had a secure hold on her, partly obscuring her view of her breast. Pain sparked through her, making her whimper.

"A beautiful sound. Now to make it happen again."

Chapter Fifteen

As he lifted her other breast off the bed, she stared at what she could see of his determination to make her his. The pain in her already-clamped breast had started to back off, making her wonder if it was more a case of her imagination than reality. Then the second clip gripped down. Whimpering, she dug her heels into the coverlet. He tightened the screws. When he'd adjusted them to his satisfaction, he grasped the connecting chain and demonstrated how he could manipulate her breasts. Fire raged in her belly. She crushed the silent vibrator between her legs while staring helplessly at her captor.

Her Master.

"Getting the point, are you?" He tugged on the chain. "Metal gives a different message than ropes do. I believe it's a deeper one."

Her attention fixed on his all-controlling hand and the flames flickering deep within her, she wondered if she'd lost a part of her mind. Not long ago, she'd wanted to be free, but that had been taken out of her hands. Only surrender was left.

And acceptance.

Wanting.

"They won't cut off all circulation," he told her. "That's why I might keep them in place for a long time. Who does your body belong to?"

In a dim way, she comprehended that her captor had asked a question, but it died beneath this demonstration of his power. She had no use of her hands and her legs were next to useless. Hell, she couldn't as much as pee without his assistance.

So that's what surrender feels like.

"My body belongs to you, Master."

"Yes. You're mine."

And that impacted him in ways she might not ever fully understand. As much as she wanted to comprehend the changes she was undergoing, she wished she could climb inside his head. Had he always had a need to dominate, or was this a relatively new development and thus one he hadn't yet made his peace with?

"Life is filled with compromise and disappointment," he said as he released the chain. "All those years I spent in school, I thought I was preparing myself for a career I could take pride in. One where I could make a difference. It didn't turn out that way."

She wanted to tell him she'd had her share of disappointments during her early working years, which was why she'd decided to become her own boss, but listening to him was more important.

That, and wondering when he'd go from words to action.

Maybe he'd read her mind, because he picked up a leather flogger and dragged the strands over her middle.

"A man can only take reality so much, only deal with the dregs of society so long before it gets to him and he decides to change things. To be in control."

Maybe she should've been used to bursts of sexual excitement charging through her by now, but he'd just introduced something new to the mix. Needing to learn what the flogger was capable of, she rolled onto her back, exposing even more of her body to him.

He bared his teeth. "Hungry little slave, aren't you? Time to see if you have what it takes."

Changing position had caused the vibrator to slip away from her core.

"Yeah," he muttered. "Yeah."

His teeth remained exposed as he slipped his free hand between her legs. After removing the vibrator, he pressed his fingers against her pussy. He didn't comment about what he'd found. She could only hope her expression spelled out how much she wanted the toy back in place.

He cocked the arm holding the flogger and struck her on her navel. The leather strands stung. Before the sensation faded, he whipped her there again. A third blow distracted her from the fingers on her sex.

"Having second thoughts about presenting yourself the way you did? Contemplate that for a while as…"

The pace picked up until there was no pause in the strikes. He targeted her belly, turning it so sensitive she felt as if she'd been scraped raw there. She'd made a fatal mistake by putting so much weight on her arms because now she could only rock a little from side to side. The chain jiggled constantly, sending sensation deep into her nipples and beyond. She started panting, quick bursts of sound that never caught up to the flogger's rhythm.

She was relieved when he started attacking her thighs, but she could hardly relax. He put more strength behind the blows, gradually increasing the impact and pushing her into a place between simply experiencing and overdrive. The stinging-biting on her trembling legs seized more and more of her attention. She wanted to say something, anything, but couldn't put her mind to what that might be. Master was drowning her, taking her deep, not hurting her as much as overwhelming her.

Somewhere in the middle of the storm-like blows, she found a wave and started riding it. Yes, she was under attack with her flesh burning, but there was something almost peaceful about it, a totality of experience. She continued to breathe like a racehorse and discomfort raged through her breasts. Rarely, when he gave her an instant of quiet, she acknowledged she had no way out. She'd continue to drown until he decided otherwise.

"Who owns you now?" He whipped the outside of her left breast, just missing the clamp.

"You. You!"

A twin of that blow struck her right breast. "No question about it?"

"No!" She hated and loved the admission.

"Wish you were anywhere but here?" The leather strands curled around the chain, shocking both breasts at the same time.

"I don't know. Master, I don't know."

A grunting chuckle from him made her wonder what he was thinking. He planted the whip lengthwise between her breasts with the chain trapped under it.

"Get off the bed."

Every move she made spoke to her imprisoned nipples and brought tears to her eyes. They'd been easier to ignore when she had been being whipped. She wasn't surprised when he didn't compliment her for doing as he'd commanded. What she didn't understand was whether he was using silence to show her who was in charge or because he'd mentally gone to a place where words had little meaning. He made a circling gesture, indicating he expected her to turn her back to him. Once she was in place, she tried to glance over her shoulder, but the collar against her neck made her think better of it.

He released her wrists and dropped the rope on the bed next to the other things he intended to use on her. He picked up something she couldn't see.

"Look at me."

She wanted to and yet she didn't, needed to fill her senses with this powerful, bare-chested man even as she emotionally mourned the lack of humanity in his eyes. He stared at her for a long time, his gaze laying bare every inch of her.

"Arms out. Inner wrists together."

Trapped by the collar and metal attached to her breasts, she complied. She'd already noticed that he had hold of a strip of leather with a buckle. This was no belt. She just wasn't sure what it was. When he placed it around her wrists and cinched the leather tightly, she had no choice but to accept yet another restraint. A metal ring much like what was imbedded into the collar was attached to it. She could move her arms up and down and from side to side but her hands were essentially useless — except that she could have removed the nipple clamps if she dared.

Or wanted to.

Waiting for the next order like the caged creature she'd become, she focused on a spot over his shoulder so she wouldn't be tempted to search his features for something that wasn't there.

"More to be done," he muttered. "Much more. A never-ending…"

Leaving the words to hang in the humid air, he walked her to the middle of the room by pulling on the nipple chain. Compliant and anxious, she hurried to keep up. He positioned her under a chain with a hook at the end which was dangling from the ceiling. After granting her nipples some relief by letting go of the thin silver, he lifted her arms over her head and attached the wrist restraint to the hook. She could stand flat-footed but move only a few inches in any direction.

Leaving her, he returned to the window, where he stood with his back to her, his shoulders squared and his face angled so the wind and rain slammed into him. After maybe a minute, he faced her. Except for being wetter than when he'd strung her up, nothing had changed about him. His dark eyes said he was in another place.

She felt so helpless, at his mercy, her body utterly exposed.

Alive. Damn, damn alive.

He crouched and unfastened his sandals and kicked them to a corner. When he started in on the zipper, her mouth filled with moisture. The task completed, he pulled the garment down over his hips. Whimpering under her breath, she clamped her legs together.

It was going to happen. She just didn't know when.

He wore white briefs that caressed his non-existent belly, buttocks, hips and, most important, his cock. The way he went about dispensing with his clothes confused her. This was no striptease, no erotic unveiling. He simply didn't want to be dressed anymore.

His cock. Big and hard. A spear at her. Dark balls surrounded by a dusting of hair.

Long before she could handle seeing him naked, he stepped away from the discarded garments and headed, not toward her, but back to the bed. He cradled his cock yet seemed barely aware of it.

What kind of man is he?

She swallowed, but her mouth again filled with saliva. Maybe it wouldn't be so hard if she could see what he was doing, but she had only his back to stare at as he sorted through the items on the bed.

Chapter Sixteen

Her captor had taken her to a spot far from their clans. He'd waited until night to further ensure that no one would intervene. With the moon guiding him, he'd strung her up to a tree branch and gagged her by forcing rope into her mouth and tying it tightly.

"You're my slave," he told her as he cut a switch from a nearby tree. "Your people pray I'll free you and return you to them, but that isn't going to happen. You belong to me. I can do whatever I want, turn you into what I need."

He wrapped rope around her waist and between her legs, cinching it so it dug into her labia and captured her clit. Ignoring her whimpers, he started slapping her breasts. When she tried to turn from him, he clamped hold of one breast, easily holding her in place. Open-handed blows pummeled her other breast. Then he switched his hold and repeated the process until she hung with her eyes closed and head back.

"You're a sexual creature," he said. "That's your downfall and what ensures my power over you.

Despite drowning in sensation, she tried to shake her head. He pulled the rope out of her mouth, grasped her jaw until she had no choice but to acknowledge him and tightened the crotch rope.

"Don't. Please don't!" she begged, but he gave her just a momentary respite before slapping her pussy.

This time she didn't say anything, felt nothing except for the sexual attack. He repeatedly focused on her crotch, watching her the whole time. Her body was aflame, his prisoner. She cried, not from pain or fear, even, but because she couldn't stop him. She was his. Everything was about his power and control and her weakness.

Her helplessness.

She returned his gaze. Everything was about her body – her helpless and aroused body.

Yes, aroused. Caught in desire and need.

Desperate to have the crotch rope gone and his fingers in its place.

His cock inside her.

* * * *

"The storm," the man she'd been calling Master said. "I don't understand it."

With an effort, she shut down her fantasy and returned to the here and now. She wasn't in the middle of a jungle, after all, but inside a cabin built for sexual pleasure.

"Don't understand it?" she asked. "What do you mean?"

He studied her as if he had no idea what she was talking about. She thought about trying to explain, but he had hold of another leather strap and was swinging it back and forth. This one appeared more substantial than what he'd used on her.

Instead of putting it to use, he dropped it on the floor at her feet and went back to the bed. When he returned, he was carrying a large black vibrator. He aimed it at her sex.

"What – ?" she started, then decided to let things play out. One thing she had no doubt of, he intended to place it inside her. Fortunately, she was well-lubricated.

"You know what you're supposed to do, slave."

She had two choices. She could either spread her legs or clamp them together. No matter what she decided, the end result would be the same. Judging by his tight hold on the dildo, he was impatient. He wanted to do what he wanted to do and she'd better comply.

Her breasts were so damn sensitive, and having her arms secured over her head had taken her far from the woman she'd been when she'd first learned about MSDB.

"You're supposed to ask what I want," she stalled. "You haven't done that."

He shrugged, pressed the dildo against her belly and turned it on. A sweet buzzing sensation chased over her. A great deal of the energy settled between her legs. The vibrator was in charge, compelling her to do what she could do to try to increase her pleasure.

Resenting Master's easy command of her, she widened her stance.

"More. This isn't a damn game."

Then what was it? Trepidation slammed against sexual heat. Almost of their own will, her legs closed an inch, then another.

"No, damn it!" With the vibrator still buzzing against her flesh, he ground a thumb into the inside of her left thigh. She gave way before his assault, cursing under her breath as she again widened her stance.

He said nothing about her compliance pleasing him. In fact, once again, he seemed barely aware of her as a separate human being. Maybe he disassociated himself from the 'clients' so he could concentrate on his dominant role, but maybe something else was working on him—something associated with the storm.

"You were given to me," he said as he took the tool on a slow journey to her pussy. "As both a gift and a test."

"Who are you talking about?" she risked asking. Now wasn't the time to remind him of the contract she'd signed. It didn't matter to him.

"I don't know. Some—something."

That made no sense, had nothing to do with what she believed BDSM was about. Much as she needed to get through to him, he wasn't in a place she could reach. If he hurt her she'd scream and cry and pray her reactions would reach him.

Not hurt, not now.

She looked down past her trapped breasts, hoping to see, as well as feel, the instrument now centered against her. The rapid-fire humming radiated over her pussy lips and she sighed in anticipation. She couldn't stop him. No matter what she said or did, if he wanted to place the tool inside her it would happen.

She wanted the same thing.

He seemed to take forever getting it into position for insertion. No matter that she sank down as best she could, in an effort to bring her sex closer to the tool, the same slow march continued.

"Not fair. Oh, God, this isn't fair." Casting caution to the wind, she shook her breasts at him. All that accomplished was to make the chain jiggle. In the past, it had hurt whenever the chain moved but now, and maybe because she was so caught up in needing to be plugged, discomfort became something else.

Something good.

Fascinated, she again shook her upper body, while keeping the rest of her open and still for him. She felt like laughing, like proclaiming herself the winner because she'd found a way to enhance her pleasure.

"I know what you're doing." He slapped her belly. "You think you've taken things into your own hands. Time to demonstrate how wrong you are."

Concern nibbled at her, but it came in a poor second to the delicious warmth radiating to all parts of her. She kept on shaking herself.

He slapped her again. "You're going to regret that."

Still lost in sensation, she locked her gaze on him. He was beautiful, amazingly male, all naked strength, maybe aware of nothing except her and his use for her.

He reached between her legs and separated her labia. When her opening was exposed to his satisfaction, he inserted the vibrator. It pounded her inner walls, invading and breaking her down.

Desperate to have some say in what was happening, she yanked at her bonds, but her arms remained over her head. Clamps still claimed her nipples and her thigh muscles burned from the splayed position. Even more all-consuming than the other sensations was how the battery-powered hard plastic felt as he guided it into her. It was eating her, taking her inch by inch, diving deep. With every second that passed, she became more aware of the vibrations. They lapped at her vagina, that so-vulnerable part of her.

"Not fair," she whimpered, while doing nothing to try to expel the invader. "Not the hell fair."

"I know."

Was there a hint of humanity in his words? As he pressed his hand over her pussy to keep the vibrator inside her, she strained to read his expression, but she'd lost too much of the ability to concentrate.

All about sex. Everything geared to — what?

"Legs together." He pressed his palm against the vibrator's base. "Keep it inside you."

She could do that. Wasn't she already panting and digging her toes into the floor as relentless movement took her closer to that delicious edge? Only one part of her body mattered. Even Master became unimportant.

He stepped back as she erased the space between her legs. Her thighs touched and she focused on not letting the invader slide out. It wasn't easy, because her channel was so slippery. Between that and gravity, she was forced to squeeze until her thigh muscles trembled. Having a job, this job, to do took her focus from her impending climax. He was putting her through what might've been an exercise in futility for her and an excuse for him to punish her, but she couldn't see any way out.

The vibrations hammering at her senses were everything, a reason for living.

Despite her effort, the vibrator slipped out just a little. Startled, she again looked down at herself then up at the naked man watching with his arms folded over his chest and his expression remote.

"It's going — I can't help it." She indicated her crotch. "It won't stay in."

"I gave you your orders. Don't defy me."

Defiance had nothing to do with losing her hold on the

toy. Maybe if he shut it down. Only she desperately needed this to continue.

"Help me, please," she begged. "You can — if you want it to stay there you'll have to secure it."

"Don't tell me what I have to do."

His voice was low, too low. Soft, but with steel behind it. Despite her turmoil, she should try to make sense of what was taking place inside him. One thing she knew, he didn't like being commanded — and not just by her.

Instead of trying to convince him that hadn't been her intention, she tightened her thigh muscles even more. The vibrator stopped withdrawing, but that would last only as long as she held out. The burning in her legs was so intense now. Much longer and it would become everything.

"Master, please." She again jerked her head at her pussy. "I don't want to anger you but —"

"You'll pay for it if you do."

With another beating. She didn't need him to spell anything out for her to understand. She was his pet, his animal, his slave, all those things and more. As such, he could do whatever he wanted to her.

He studied her a little longer then picked up the leather strap. His gaze hard on her, he forced his free hand between her legs and shoved the vibrator back into her. She shuddered when he snaked the strap around her thighs and tightened it so her legs were jammed together.

"I've been putting off the true test." He fiddled with something. The vibrations increased. "This is high."

With the tool attacking her like a dog shaking a toy, she couldn't focus on anything else. Besides, why should she try? She was being fucked. The vibrator lacked the warmth and life of a cock, but her pussy didn't care. The strap around her thighs kept the invader deep within her. As long as the batteries held out, she'd remain in its grip.

After watching her shake and stare for a while, Master went back to the bed. She tried to see what he was after but her nerves demanded so much from her. This felt so damn good.

Overwhelming, exhausting and full of messages about helplessness.

"What are—how long—?" She stared at his spine, his buttocks, willing him to acknowledge her. "What is the point of...?"

She was drenched in sweat and gasping with every breath by the time he faced her again. Acknowledging what his cock represented should have distracted her from the never-ending stimulation, but she couldn't break free. Why didn't he tell her how to wrench back control, damn it? Maybe he thought this was funny, but he was wrong. She couldn't make the movements stop and now dreaded being kept in suspended ecstasy and agony.

"Please," she whimpered. "Please. I'll— What do you want me to do? Anything. Anything." She wrenched her body to the left then to the right but found no escape.

"You don't get it, do you? There's nothing you can do. I'm in charge."

Chapter Seventeen

He was holding a whip. Why hadn't she noticed it before?

Suddenly, she felt as if she were drowning. The mindless part of her that responded to pleasure and discomfort kept dancing to the tune of the batteries locked inside her, but the thin, flexible switch took hold of her brain.

He was going to hurt her with it.

"Why?" She couldn't do more than whisper. "What have I done to deserve—?"

"You came here because you wanted to experience life as a sub, remember? You're getting what you wanted, so don't the hell complain."

He had it all wrong. No way could she survive the extremes of stimulation. She frowned when he snapped his fingers. Then he did it again and comprehension replaced confusion. He wanted her to stand still, expected her to obey as a well-trained dog would.

Turning from side to side had kept the forced stimulation from overwhelming her. Now, as she shivered in place, she acknowledged that a new emotion had come into play. She was afraid, not of the pain as much as her inability to handle everything he meted out.

"Time to change things up a bit." He extended his hand toward her breasts. "To see how you handle this."

He didn't care about her comfort. If he did, she wouldn't have been strung up the way she was. She'd been handed over to a man without an ounce of humanity in him. A Master who thought of himself as a conquering warrior and she his helpless hostage.

His slave in every sense of the word.

All those thoughts and more passed through her in the time it took him to close a thumb and forefinger over the screw that kept the clamp locked on her nipple. Her pussy throbbed and her clit ached, threatening to distract her from what Master was doing.

Master, she acknowledged once again. The man who ruled every part of her existence.

Studying her, he loosened the screw and drew the clamp off her. Blood rushed back into her nipple.

"That—hurts so." She stared at her now purple flesh. If only she could've rolled into a ball and protected herself there.

He roughly massaged her breast. "That's the point."

She wanted to tell him he had it wrong. Nipple clamps had been designed for sexual pleasure, but he was talking about what he expected from the exercise. By the time he'd finished fingering her flesh, the pins and needles sensation was all but gone. She closed her eyes as he reached for her other breast and tried to go somewhere in her mind. Her attempt to distract herself didn't work.

"Hurt," she said as he released the clamp. "You hurt me."

He slapped her cheek. "Don't take off on me. I want you here." He slapped her other cheek. Neither blow was hard, just enough to get her attention.

Eyes wide open, she suffered through the stinging in her nipple until she could breathe without gasping. If he was pleased with her ability to handle pain, he gave no indication. Now that that experience was behind her, she wondered when he'd again command her breasts. Maybe he had other clamps at his disposal, perhaps a gold set with a heavier chain and weights to hang from it or the clamps themselves.

Maybe he'd parade her before the other Doms here—or make her stand in front of the members of her tribe or clan with proof of his mastery imbedded in her flesh.

He might even brand her or pierce her nipples and fasten rings through the holes he'd created.

Teach her what it meant to be owned.

Wondering if he could guess what she was thinking, she blinked. He still held the whip.

"I mentioned this before," he said. "I'm not interested in belaboring the point. All you need to do is remember that under the right conditions and with the right Dom doing the work, there's an unbreakable link between pleasure and pain. The two become one in your mind. Either, or both, will reach you."

He started whipping her. The slender lash laid down lines of fire over her torso. She tugged on her bonds and tried to kick him, but he'd done an expert job of restraining her. Whether she stood flat-footed or rose onto her toes made no difference. She couldn't lower her arms or get out of his reach. The leather now biting into her thighs held her. She wasn't going anywhere.

Neither could she take herself beyond the whipping. No matter how hard she tried to return to the simple world where two primitive societies fought over water rights, she couldn't. During those too-brief moments when the lash didn't sting her buttocks, breasts or belly, she imagined herself trudging naked behind her mounted Master, her wrists connected by rope to a saddle horn. The primitive human was taking her to a place her people didn't know about. As the conquering warrior, he rode. As his slave, she walked.

The whip sharply kissed the top of one breast, followed by the other and pulled her back to the room. For too long, there was nothing to her except trying to endure. Then what was taking place between her legs became paramount.

Slave to passion.

Slave to passion.

It didn't matter where or even if she'd heard that before or how purple the prose. For her, now, it was real.

Wonderfully so.

"I've got you where I want you." He lashed the front of her thighs. "Right where you deserve to be."

Yes, she nearly admitted. This—this thing was what she needed. Her skin wasn't being broken, but even if it was, she wasn't sure she'd care. Her nerves were on overload. A tumbling, thrashing confusion centered in her pussy.

"This is all you're good for." He stepped behind her and began striking her buttocks. "The reason you're alive. Who am I? Who the hell am I?"

"Master," she bleated past the earthquake inside her. "My Master."

He whipped her from high on her buttocks nearly to her knees, one blow right after the other so it all ran together. "What does a slave do to express her gratitude?"

"I don't—?" Her pussy seized hold of the vibrator, refused to let go. "Whatever you want."

"I'm not going to spell it out." He came around in front and grabbed her chin. "How do you thank me for beating and pleasuring you?"

"I can't—" She pulled on the overhead chain. Was he going to strike her again? "I want to, ah, give you head but I can't."

He actually seemed surprised when she said that and his hold on her chin let up a little. They were so close, both of them sweating. Now that her ass was no longer under assault, the vibrations locked inside her threatened to take over. She could've spent the rest of her life like this.

"I don't believe you." He sounded disappointed. "Maybe later, once you're fully trained, but it's too soon for any novice to make the offer you just did."

Was it? She didn't know. In fact, she wasn't sure she could do what she'd just offered to. Maybe if the vibrator—

But it was still going and she'd become its willing slave.

Her body started to gather itself. The wonderful helpless explosion was a heartbeat away. Lost in her impending climax, she reached out and touched her lips to her Master's. She moaned in response to his answering kiss then shattered. She jerked and screamed, fought to stop because she was giving too much away.

"That's what this is about." He shoved her away from him, stepped back and teased her breasts with the whip he handled so well. "Owning you. Claiming you."

He hadn't acknowledged the slave crumpled at his feet since letting her down. He heard her ragged breathing and the sound her nails made as they dug at the wooden floor, so he knew she was all right—all right being a relative term.

Damn, but she was responsive. Even though he'd taken a number of women on this ride or one close to it, he could only speculate about what she'd undergone. A few of the women had tried to explain. They'd thrown out words like 'hurricane' or likened the collision of pleasure and pain to downhill skiing with no way of stopping.

He wasn't sure he'd want to feel that way. Being in control was vital to him. What was it he'd told his parents when he'd been going through his rebellious teenage years—that he could hardly wait to be twenty-one so he'd be in charge of his life? Once he was, he'd do what he wanted, when he wanted and no one could tell him differently. He'd said they were wrong when his parents had told him he wouldn't feel that way once he'd been an adult for a while.

Now he knew how right they'd been.

He pushed his toe into her side and shook his head when she tried to swat it away. Before letting her down, he'd gotten rid of the thigh strap and pulled the drenched vibrator out of her. He'd left her wrists tied with her palms together because, even in the aftermath of what had been one hell of a climax, he didn't want her to forget who was in charge.

His cock was.

A groan escaped him. If she'd heard, she gave no indication. Leaving her with her thoughts, he strode back to the window. Summer storms here seldom lasted long, but this one showed no sign of ending. Thunder continued its deep rumblings and lightning snapped. He'd hesitated about returning to the island because it held some power over him, but that paled in contrast to the storm's strength. As a child, he'd been in awe of what nature was capable of. As the years passed, he'd stopped being intimidated by downpours. Then he'd come here for the first time. In the process of embracing the Dominant in him, he'd become aware of wind and clouds. He hadn't told anyone about losing his grip on the man who spent his days enforcing the law. The other MSDB Doms and management saw him as an established practitioner of the BDSM lifestyle. They didn't know how hard it was for him to shove the beast back into its cave or his fear of the next time the creature was unleashed.

Don't let it win. Don't lose yourself.

A thunderclap buried the command. By the time he again noted rain striking the building and trees, his world had changed. He was no longer looking at the vegetation just beyond the cabin. His surroundings had changed into a tangle of lush growth with a thin trail threading through it.

Imagination—if that's what it was—took over. He felt rough ground beneath his feet and the occasional slap of leaves, branches and vines as they struck his naked flesh. The music of insects and birds filled his ears. The air was heavy with the scent of rampant growth.

He didn't know or care where he was going, just that today's tasks included walking along this path. More would be revealed once he reached his destination. In the meantime, he lived in the moment.

Predator. Captor.

The words tightened his muscles. Filled with anticipation, he stared at his surroundings but saw nothing he'd consider worthy prey for a hunter like him.

Something tugged at his hand. Rope was wrapped around it. More stretched out behind him.

Smiling with his teeth clenched, he yanked on the rope. A naked woman stumbled toward him.

What had led to this moment didn't matter. Only taking things forward did. His deadly grin in place, he studied his prisoner. Her dark hair stuck to her sweaty cheeks, forehead and neck while her dazed eyes left no doubt that she was tired. Wooden doweling was jammed between her teeth, held in place by strapping that went behind her head. Someone—him—had fashioned a crude bridle for her to wear.

She was naked with upright breasts, a slender waist and hips a man could lose himself in. Her hands were tied in front, palm to palm. She couldn't lift her arms because more rope snaked around her waist and between her legs, connected to what was around her wrists. Obviously, he'd been dragging her after him.

His plan, his secret and dark plan was to take her somewhere for his use. To turn her into what the beast in him needed.

No! Don't give in!

Somehow.

His body tight, hard and hot, he presented the wilderness with his back and fought to destroy what existed only in his sick, helpless mind. The battle tested his strength but finally he completed the journey back to reality.

The woman who'd paid good money so he'd tease her with a taste of what submission and Dominance meant again came into focus. She was sitting up, staring at him as if she'd never seen anything like him—and wanted him.

Don't let the devil win!

Somehow.

Chapter Eighteen

The Devil was in him.

Shock yanked Shana out of the dark pool she'd been swimming in. She still felt as if she'd been in a wreck and would've given a great deal to have use of her hands, but those things came in second to studying the man walking toward her.

Earlier, she'd likened him to a predator. The label still fit. She wouldn't be surprised if he grew fangs and claws, or if he charged her.

Driven into action by his stalking stride, she awkwardly pushed herself to her feet. Her pussy muscles felt stretched, as if the vibrator was still inside her while her nerves replayed the sensations that had sent her over the edge.

Master stopped, slipped a hand under his erection and aimed it at her. He said nothing. Thinking he might be ordering her to suck on it, she studied the living room with its open door.

Reality again faded as she envisioned herself running through the jungle with him in pursuit. She'd somehow broken free. Filled with emotions that threatened to swamp her, she pounded along the crushed seashell path.

She was naked, of course, with her hands bound in front. Every step caused what was between her legs to rub against her labia and clit. A length of rope bounced along the ground behind her, threatening to trip her.

When she tried to scream, she discovered she'd been gagged with a length of smooth wood.

"It won't do you any good," her pursuer said. *"Run all you want, you'll never get away."*

He sounded so fresh and strong. In contrast, her lungs burned and her legs were about to give out. She had no idea where she was or whether this path would lead to freedom. For all she knew, other men like him were waiting around the next turn. If so, they'd throw her to the ground and hold her down until Master caught up. Once he had her again, he'd haul her back to her cage where — where what?

"You've had enough time to rest," the man sharing the cabin with her said. "Back to getting your money's worth."

Wishing he'd put off touching her until she'd brought her mind back to what was real, she lifted her arms and fingered her collar. She wasn't gagged after all. No rope trapped her hands at her waist. "What if I said I don't need to experience anything else? Maybe you've satisfied my curiosity."

"You might be done, but I'm not."

"You?" She couldn't comprehend what was going on inside him. Seconds ago, he'd sounded exactly like she'd expected a paid Dom to, full of concern for her wellbeing and interested in pleasing her. That impression had changed. Now it was all about him. If she was lucky, both of them would come out of this as winners. If not —

"Sit down." He jerked his head at the hard chair which lacked a decent seat.

"What if I don't want to?"

His eyes glittered. "It won't make any difference."

She'd already suspected that, so why had she goaded him? Maybe she was stalling, delaying learning what he had in mind. At least he'd given her a choice, she reminded herself as she tried to settle on the strange-feeling device. Its design was, basically, like a toilet except it was higher off the ground and a box was under the opening.

Not waiting for her to finish moving around, he pulled her arms over her head and attached her wrists to yet another hanging chain. Her elbows were positioned so she couldn't see past them. He kneeled in front of her and placed leather strapping around both ankles. When he had it tightened to his liking, he pulled her legs out to either side of the chair and up so they were off the ground. He fastened the strapping to the chair legs.

"What's going to happen?" she asked as he stood up. "At least tell me that."

"It won't make any difference."

Stop saying that! "Because, no matter what I say, you're going to do what you want?"

"Yeah."

One word shouldn't have carried so much meaning and maybe her imagination was getting away from her, but it was as if he'd distanced himself from her. If she told him about her crazy flight of fantasy of trying to run away from him would he say he'd been there himself?

When he stepped behind her, she swiveled her head, hoping to see what he was up to, but her damned arms prevented that. She surmised he was doing something at the back of the chair. Why hadn't she thought to check it out when she'd had the opportunity? Yes, the sight of him had mesmerized her, but that was no excuse. The next time he left her alone she'd —

Something passed in front of her eyes. Just like that, he robbed her of the ability to see.

"No!" Alarmed, she bucked.

"Yes, slave, yes."

"No!" She struggled to get out of the chair but, with her legs elevated and her arms restrained, she couldn't lift herself off the non-seat. Being thrust into darkness was an overwhelming sensation. She'd been robbed of a vital sense. Her helplessness doubled.

"Why?" she begged as he tightened the blindfold. "Please, why are you doing this?"

He stroked her uplifted arms. "Go deep into yourself. Let your body speak to you."

Fear still threatened her sanity. At the same time, she realized he understood what she was going through emotionally. Every time he did something different she became even more off balance and dependent on him. Now, it didn't matter that he'd blinded her and robbed her of the ability to move. They shared the same space, and that was everything.

"I watched you at work the other day," he said.

A deep tremor slashed through her. "You did? I didn't see —"

"Because I didn't want you to." He nipped at her right shoulder blade, making her scream. "I needed to see if you were worth it." He raked his teeth over her left shoulder blade. She shrieked. "I decided you were."

He was tearing her apart, damn him! Forcing her into some deep pit. "Worth it?"

"The risk to me — risk versus reward."

He must have taken hold of the ring at the back of her collar, because her head was being forced forward and down. Was he looking at her neck like a vampire would? Maybe he was wondering what her blood tasted like.

I'm scared. You scare me so.

"That isn't your concern." He continued to immobilize her head. "I shouldn't let it get to me but…"

She forced her way through the thick fog surrounding her. "You're wrong. I want to understand."

"Too late."

* * * *

Shock after shock flooded her senses. She was drowning again, going down deep once more. The vibrator he'd placed in her vagina had been on the move for so long she couldn't think back to when it had started. At first, the variations had thrilled her. She'd delighted in the contrast between tiny flutterings and fierce shaking, the uneven spacing between the extremes and everything in between. She'd surmised that the unseen invader was powered by electricity, which meant it could, and might, outlast her.

She could no longer distinguish between the differences.

When the movements slipped off to nearly nothing she struggled to suck the tool further into her. When it pounded at her, she strained to escape.

That was when everything became too much. She wasn't sure, but thought she climaxed each time the vibrations were on overdrive. No matter that she hated letting him know the depths of her helplessness, she couldn't stay silent. Over and over again, she begged him to release her, but he didn't heed her desperate pleas. And he whipped her.

Breasts, mostly her breasts, but sometimes her legs and belly. Whatever he was using had three or four slender strands. They found her nerve endings, opened them up and flung them into the universe.

"Can't stand, can't stand—Master, please—please, I can't—I don't…"

"Don't talk. Experience."

She already had. Thinking this might go on until she fainted was more than she could handle. In desperation, she resolved to focus on her climaxes. No matter that she'd already gone beyond the point of exhaustion, she'd dive body and soul into those precious moments so, somehow, she'd survive the rest.

"A slave's lot." The whip slapped her right nipple then the left. "Living to please your Master, a Master who loves watching his helpless slave suffer."

"I am," she whimpered. In the beginning, she'd been determined to prove herself worthy of the man who'd taken away her freedom, but thanks to the mix of pummeled pussy and ignited breasts, she simply existed. Drowned. Climaxed. Endured.

"You think I should be proud of what you're capable of enduring?" He gripped her nipples. "You're hoping you've proven yourself."

She forced herself not to try to get free. Just then the vibrator hit overdrive. She writhed on the beast. "I don't know. Master, please, what do you want of me?"

He released her nipples. "More of this." Twin lines of pain seized her breasts as the whip came home. "You belong to me, get it? I'm in control of every sensation you experience. Good or bad, it all comes from me."

Because of him, her legs had no function. If he wanted, she'd spend hours with her arms over her head. Maybe the vibrator would never stop. He might keep her blinded until she forgot what sight was like.

His. Trapped by her stupid determination to experience something called MSDB. A prisoner of her own desires.

"Take it."

He whipped her again, this time on the outsides of her held-in-place thighs. A strange music blasted through her. It took her too long to realize she was listening to herself hum. Fascinated, she stopped begging him to stop.

She didn't know this body. It was new, a creation she'd never suspected existed. There was no world beyond this room. Only she and Master mattered. Maybe she'd never understand what drove him to do the things he did, but she had to try. He deserved something.

"Master." She all but sang the word. "My lord and Dominant."

"Who's saying that? The woman you were when you came here or what you're becoming?"

"Both. They aren't separate."

When he didn't reply, she strained to catch any sound that might tell her what he was doing. He'd stopped abusing her so-sensitive flesh, leaving her to hope he was still standing before her, watching her uncontrollable movements. The insistent vibrations tested her ability to think of anything except this. She no longer tried to anticipate when another climax might seize her or guess how she'd respond, simply thanked the all-powerful man who'd brought her to this place.

"I never guessed it would be like this," she admitted. "Had no idea — ah, yes."

This climax was gentler than most that had come before

it. It eased over her like a lazy wave, consuming her nonetheless, and continuing for a long time. She moaned in tune with it, a low breathless hiss of delight.

"What's happening?" Master asked as she sagged and experienced. "What are you feeling?"

"I can't...can't explain." Pleasure seeped into every inch of her, to silence her strained muscles and abraded skin. She imagined herself floating on a cloud, one capable of turning dark, dangerous and exciting at any moment.

His hands cupped her breasts and he massaged them. "Stay with it," he whispered. "Embrace everything and let this become part of you."

Part of her? Was he saying these feelings might last forever? Even as the small still-sane piece of her mind that remained insisted that wasn't possible, she wanted it to be wrong. Living the rest of her life drunk on sex?

"Thank you, Master," she got out.

The wave was starting to flatten, but she remained aware of the hammering inside her. Before long she'd start to drown again. Master's gentle fingers on her breasts felt so good, a wonderful contrast to what he'd been forcing them to endure earlier. She lifted her heavy head and tried to lean toward him.

"What are you doing?"

"I want to kiss you."

He took a long breath. "No. Damn it, no."

"Why not?" She didn't try to hide her begging tone.

"I'm not going to let our relationship take that turn. You're my slave, nothing more."

Chapter Nineteen

"What are you doing?"

The naked woman angled her body away from the window and looked at him. She showed no sign of wanting to leave it. After freeing her from the chair and removing the blindfold, he'd again restrained her hands behind her and told her she could use the toilet. He might not have thought about her needs in that department if he hadn't needed to pee himself. Wanting to see what, if anything, she'd do when left alone, he'd ordered her to leave the bathroom when she was done. He'd kept the door open while urinating in case she tried to run but she hadn't taken a step toward the living room.

Instead, like him, she wanted to see the still-raging storm. She didn't seem reluctant to present her face to the rain-drenched wind. He told himself that, maybe, she was hoping rain would wash off some of her sweat, but the explanation didn't go deep enough. She undoubtedly wanted more than to be clean.

"I work in all kinds of weather. Most of the time I don't think about it, but it's different today. There's something about this storm. Maybe it's the island."

It is. He studied her slight but strong frame. Being denied use of her arms hadn't reduced her in the ways that counted. Her legs were widely spread, undoubtedly because her pussy was so sensitive. Seeing how reddened her breasts were surprised him. He couldn't remember everything he'd done to them.

Acknowledging that he'd briefly — it hadn't been long, had it? — blacked out alarmed him. At the same time, he couldn't fathom ending what they'd begun today.

"I don't know what I'm supposed to say." Her attention stayed on his cock. "I-I was led to believe I'd be directing much of the, ah, action. So far that hasn't happened."

She swayed a little. He again tried to pull up the details of what had happened between them, but there were too many blank spaces. There wasn't an inch of her that didn't speak of what he'd put her through. Any man who wanted to be able to look himself in the mirror would have already ended things, handed her back her freedom.

He wasn't that man.

"Come closer," he ordered, slapping the mattress he was sitting on.

He thought she might fall but she caught herself before he had to decide whether he'd help. Judging by the strain in her shoulders, she was testing the strength of the ropes wound around her wrists.

"Now. Damn it!"

Most men probably wouldn't have seen the truth behind her uplifted head, but he knew things about women they never would. She wasn't resisting the command. Rather, the conflict was with herself.

"Tell me what you're thinking," he said.

"You'd like that, wouldn't you?" she snapped. "It isn't enough that I'm naked and tied up, you expect me to spill my guts."

"You want to." He wasn't sure where that insight came from, let alone what he might do with it.

She licked her lips. "Maybe," she muttered. "It's—"

"Not yet. First, you'll obey my command."

Watching her close the distance between them until his cock was only inches from her had him fighting not to take her here and now, but he refused to fuck her before she begged for it.

"What do you want from men?" he asked to get her started. "What would it take for you to consider a man marriage material?"

"You want me to tell you — ?" She closed her eyes. "I don't know if I can."

"Can't or won't?"

"I'm not sure."

Oh, she knew all right, damn her. Time to dig into her corners and lay her bare in ways she couldn't have anticipated. He had only one goal, to turn her into something the beast had use for.

Even if it meant destroying her?

Desperate to kill the question, he ordered her to open her eyes. When she did, he noted that they were glittering.

"What," he asked, "is the one thing you hoped no one would ever know about you?"

She shrank away. "Not fair," she whispered. "I don't have to — "

"Yeah, you do." He gave weight to the words by grasping her hips and pulling her into the space he'd created by spreading his legs. He clamped his thighs around hers. After several seconds, she rewarded him with a strained moan. He backed off the pressure but made it clear that she'd pay for it if she tried to move.

"Everyone has secrets. Things they'll never tell anyone. What gives you nightmares?"

"Nothing."

She was lying. Hell, maybe he wasn't the only one who feared the dark side would win. He could beat the truth out of her, whip and stimulate her until she didn't know what was happening, but he'd already taken her down that road. It was time for another approach.

He slipped his forefinger through the ring dangling from her collar and pulled down until she bent over at the waist. She widened her stance a bit, in an attempt to keep her balance, which was exactly what he'd intended. He kept her bracketed between his legs.

"I won't abide lies from you." The sense of power that had climbed inside him as the storm exploded returned. He didn't know this slave's name and didn't care. She was simply a means to an end.

His end?

"I know you won't. The thought of something happening to my business so I can't pay the bills sometimes keeps me up nights."

"Is that possible? Things aren't secure?" Where had the questions come from, when he'd told himself he didn't care about who she was when she wasn't with him?

"It's better than when I was starting out, but there's always competition. I can't control the weather. I've been stiffed by a few people I've completed jobs for. Even if I don't get paid, I have to pay my employees."

"Why?"

"Why?" She tried to lift her head. "They have families to feed."

And their ability to do so is important to you.

Taken aback by what he'd just learned, and what the knowledge meant to him, he tried to distract himself by running his free hand over her hip. She sighed and shuddered. For several seconds, he wasn't aware of anything except the vulnerable and lovely young woman standing helpless before him. With his ropes on her, she was dependent on him for so many things and she knew it. No matter what she might think of him, no matter that she might have labeled him a bastard, she knew not to antagonize him. She'd do whatever she believed she needed to, in order to keep him from abandoning her.

As if he would.

Had it come to that, he pondered, as he stroked her flank and thigh. This nameless woman was more than an object, more than the means to sexual release? Somehow, she'd slipped past his defenses, past the beast, even to something basic and real.

No!

He didn't know where the denial had come from, just that he needed to heed it and make that his reality.

By doing what he was so good at.

"You will *not* climax. If you do I'll punish you, understand?"

She tried to nod but it was nearly impossible because this man, who'd once again become her Master, still had hold of the collar's ring. She remained bent over, as if bowing before him with her breasts dangling. She'd briefly lost sight of their declared relationship but he'd thrown it back at her in a way she hadn't seen coming.

His fingers on her hip had been a kind of music, a cooling breeze during a hot afternoon, and she wanted it back, not this.

Master's hand was between her legs. His fingers flicked over her labia and came within a whisper of her clit. She'd been aroused even before he'd made his intentions clear and that had contributed to her downfall. His earlier bold handling of her had brought her to this place where self-determination was a lie. She wanted to loathe him for it. Instead, she was seeping into a world of helpless pleasure.

"Keeping secrets from your Master isn't allowed." He slid a finger inside her where it lingered for several seconds.

She swayed. "I don't have nightmares, if that's what you want to know."

There was nothing warm about his chuckle. "No, it isn't," he said. "I don't give a damn about what wakes you in the middle of the night. What you're going to tell me is what keeps you from falling asleep."

She couldn't imagine what he was talking about, couldn't push her mind past the warmth pressing against the inside of her left thigh.

"You're sexually unfulfilled." His fingers drummed her flesh. "You wouldn't be here if you were getting what you need."

He was right. She slipped into that hot and welcome place where nothing except sensuality mattered. Master's hand was at the only place she wanted it to be. He'd taken her where she'd hoped she'd be led. There'd been more pain and bondage than she'd anticipated, but did it matter?

"Did any of your lovers scratch your deep itches?" He punctuated the question by pushing a finger deep inside her. "Any of them ever tie you up?"

Oh, God! "No."

"Why not?"

Keep your finger there. Fill me with your essence. "I, ah, didn't ask them to."

A second finger joined the first.

"Why not, slave? Why did it take my collaring you to get you to admit what you need?"

The question was too complex. If he wanted openness from her he'd have to give her room to breathe.

"I don't know."

"I don't believe you." He bent his fingers so the tips touched a hot and hungry part of her core. "Damn it, you know who and what you are."

Did she?

"Master? What do you want from me?"

"Your soul."

Feeling as if he'd struck her, she tried to straighten, but his grip on the collar's ring made that impossible. His legs imprisoned hers and the fingers lodged in her said he had every right to claim that part of her. Even if she broke free, she couldn't go anywhere except out into the rain-battered world the island had become.

"None of your lovers touched your secret places." His invading fingers dove deeper. "That's where I'm headed. How am I doing? Getting close to the truth?"

Yes, she silently declared, even though she wasn't sure what he was talking about.

He pressed against the front of her channel. "Talk to me, slave. Spread yourself open to me. Maybe I'll give you what you need."

She needed to come again, but he'd ordered her not to let loose until he gave her permission. Thoughts of how he might punish her if she failed him had her fighting to find her way beyond her plundered pussy. "Everyone thinks I have my—my shit together," she managed. "My family's so damn proud of me it scares me."

"Why?"

Something in his tone got through to her. Even with sexual hunger clawing at her, she wanted to come clean. "I get tied in knots thinking I might fail. They don't know about the times I had to get high-interest loans to make it through the month, my fear no one would want my services."

"You wanted your family to believe you were a roaring success coming out of the chute?"

"It wasn't that," she hurried to say, even as she acknowledged he was right in too many respects.

"I don't believe you."

Why was she so tired? Yes, her body was on overdrive with desire chasing through it so she thought she might drown, but under that was a soul-deep weariness. She hadn't felt this exhausted for maybe a couple of years, not since the last time she'd feared she was in over her head.

As she hesitantly replayed the mix of anger and anxiety that had consumed her because a businessman she'd done a large project for kept delaying a much-needed payment, she acknowledged the common thread in both experiences. Too much was out of her control, so much at stake.

"You're trapped," Master said. He allowed her to straighten while continuing to invade her pussy. "You can't close down your business and hire on with some other landscaper or get an office job any more than you can pretend you never wanted to come here. Never asked to be treated the way I'm treating you."

Despite everything, she caught the continued note of genuine interest in his voice. Gathering resolve from a place outside her body, she studied him. His eyes had lightened a little, become less dangerous. More sane.

"No, I can't," she admitted.

He nodded. "And you knew that even before you embarked on either experience. Down deep you knew you were a submissive."

'Submissive'. Such a simple word. Simple and unbelievably complex.

"What about you?" she asked, to keep from blurting out the truth. "How long have you known about your need to dominate?"

"No you don't." His tone turned harsh. "We aren't going there."

He'd retreated again, gone to a place she couldn't reach. "I can't make you say anything you don't want to, but — "

"No, you can't. So, this is my take on you, little slave. You present a public face to the world and your family. They see a confident and competent kick-ass woman. They know nothing about your secret need to turn all responsibility over to someone — to a man who takes what he wants."

They'd already had a similar conversation. If only she could remember how it had played out — or whether she'd admitted how right he was.

Maybe it didn't matter.

"Not many people you'd want to see you like this, right?"

The contract she'd signed had assured complete privacy. Had she been a fool to blindly believe it would be honored?

"One more time," he said. "You'd rather die than have pictures of how you are right now make the rounds, right?"

"No." She started to back up, only to stop. If she took another step, his fingers would slide out of her. "I mean you can't — I'll sue."

"Sue who or what? Besides, you don't want the notoriety."

He was right. Once the pictures became public the damage would have been done.

"Please don't," she whispered as she returned to where she'd been.

He didn't respond as he settled his fingers more firmly inside her, studying her as he did. Something in his expression warned of more to come. He could hurt or pleasure her at will, both at the same time if he so desired. His erection served as the only sign that arousal was a two-edged sword.

"Quite the day of revelations, isn't it?" Fresh pressure against her labia made deciding whether he expected her to respond impossible. "You never thought there'd be so much mind fucking."

A third finger slowly made its way into her already stuffed channel. Her thoughts locked on the hard invasion. She heard herself pant.

"You can leave if you want to." He placed his free hand on her hip and pressed his fingers against her ass cheek to anchor her in place. "Turn around and walk out the door."

"I can't." She arched toward him, moving her upper body about so her breasts shook. "You have— I can't."

"Yes, you can. Go on, back away." He removed his hand from her buttock, holding it up so she could see it out of the corner of her eye. "I'll slide right out." He made his point by withdrawing his fingers a little. "All you have to do is make the decision."

"My arms—they're cuffed."

"Don't let that stop you. Don't forget, the moment you say you've had enough someone will get you out of the mess you've gotten yourself into."

He was right. "What do you want me to do? To say?"

The hint of a teasing expression she'd spotted, while he was challenging her, died. "Listen to yourself? You're asking me what you should be thinking."

He was right. Down in her bones right. Exhaustion again threatened to take over. "Yes," she admitted. "I'm so tired of— I don't want to think anymore."

"Another layer exposed." He patted her flank. "More honesty held up to the light."

But it was all one-sided because he'd said so little about himself. Somehow, she pulled energy from some deep place. Careful not to dislodge his hand, she bent at the waist and brought her face close to his. His exhaled breath dampened her lashes.

"Kiss me," she whispered. "That's what I want, for you

to kiss me."

The change in his expression reminded her of a dog going from being remote to on the verge of attacking. Shock froze her breath.

"That's not the way things work here, slave." He gripped her chin. "This is no damn romantic getaway."

"Then what is it?" she snapped. *What the hell just happened?*

"What I need it to be."

Not 'want' but 'need'. The longer they stared at each other the more convinced she became that he wasn't in control of what he was experiencing. Granted, this wasn't the first time she'd thought that, but now she believed they were getting closer. That she was catching glimpses of the man who existed beyond this place and this storm.

She groaned and fought to clamp his fingers inside her. He too easily slipped free, leaving her on the verge of screaming.

"What is it, slave?" He slapped her breasts. "Your clan's men ordered you to use your body to disarm your captor? You believed you could break me down, distract me from the threat of danger?"

He didn't sound like himself. That, coupled with the distrust radiating out from him, said he'd stepped fully into what she'd thought had been fantasy play.

"I had to try, Master." She lowered her gaze. "I'm at your mercy. You can kill me. I don't dare forget that."

Still holding her chin, he roughly fingered her stinging breasts. Between that manipulation and her on-fire pussy, she could barely think.

"I don't want you dead. You're useful to me now."

Alerted by the strange, almost primitive tone, she continued her submissive stance. "In what way, Master? I want to please you, but—"

"Prove it."

Chapter Twenty

She was a lovely creature. Her helplessness spoke to him as nothing ever had. He'd bound her wrists in front, leaving enough distance between them that she could have removed her blindfold. Instead, she'd willingly let him lead her outside via a short leash hooked to her collar. He'd guided her down the stairs and along the path leading to the building where MSDB clients and employees took their meals. He hadn't bothered to tell her what he had in mind, not because her need to eat mattered to him, but because everyone was required to appear in public every few hours.

The truth was, he wasn't sure why he'd led his slave into this area with cameras and an assortment of food and drinks set out on a long table. Although they were the only ones there, he sensed eyes on him as he positioned her near the table and ordered her onto her knees.

She moved her head about. The way she kept raising her hands toward her face told him how hard remaining blind was. He hadn't spoken to her since repositioning her bonds, hadn't explained that robbing her of sight and making her dependent on him was designed to both test her subservience and fill him with an even greater sense of power.

This naked female at his feet belonged to him. She ate when he decided to feed her, walked where he compelled her to go, spoke when he gave permission.

He glanced at the camera set high in a corner then dismissed it. As long as he and his captive were left alone, he didn't care what anyone saw or thought.

The smell of barbequed beef made his mouth water. He

selected a slice off a large plate and chewed. The food was his due, provided for him by his grateful people because he was a skilled warrior and hunter. He ate another slice then held a turkey leg in both hands and gnawed on it. Instead of using a napkin to wipe his fingers, he ran them through his captive's hair. She sank lower and dropped her head a little.

He bumped her shoulder with his knee. "Are you hungry, slave?"

"Yes, Master."

"But you can't reach the food, can you?" Not waiting for a reply, he picked up the leash dangling between her breasts and tugged to let her know he expected her to crawl closer to him. "Think about that, slave. Admit how dependent you are on me."

"I know — at least I'm trying to understand."

Despite her quiet words, he didn't believe her. She was the enemy. If she had a chance, she'd run back to her people. She might even try to kill him.

The thought of her attacking him made him smile. Surely, she understood she didn't stand a chance against his greater strength, but the instinct for survival made people, even fully trained and cowed slaves, take dangerous chances.

Maybe he'd fool her into thinking she could escape. He'd pretend to fall asleep without first securing her. Then he'd wait and watch. No matter whether she sprinted for the door or went in search of a weapon, he'd teach her the error of her ways. He'd punish her so —

But not too much. He had no use for a slave whose spirit had been broken. Men worthy of the name didn't do that to weak rivals.

The room seemed to shrink. Now that he'd filled his belly, he wanted to return to the wilderness, where he belonged. He drew his fingers out of the slave's hair and ran them over her blindfold. She'd done what he'd ordered her to, hadn't resisted or complained since he'd robbed her of sight. He could put off escaping these walls long enough to feed her.

Still gripping the leash, he selected a slice of apple and touched it to her lips. The sound of chewing briefly ended the silence. When she was done, she tried to rub her cheek against him.

"What is it, pet? Asking for more food, are you?"

"Yes, Master, please."

Did it please him to feed her, or should he use the moment to teach her even more about his control over her? Thinking that she might have trouble concentrating with a growling stomach, he gave her the rest of the apple, followed by orange slices. Next, he selected a cracker with cheese on it. As she ate, he pondered whether he'd been too kind to her. Maybe he should have fed her something tasteless or foul-tasting.

Deciding she'd had enough, he opened a water bottle and tapped her lips with it. Watching her drink, he tried to remember how and when she'd come into his possession but couldn't.

Maybe once the storm was over.

Maybe if his thinking cleared.

And if not—

Then he'd keep her forever.

* * * *

Not being able to see where she was going was unnerving enough, but Master's dark silence made the walk through the downpour even worse. She wished he'd given her more to eat but at least those bites had demonstrated he hadn't completely gotten lost in whatever had overtaken him.

She should have called out for help when they had been in wherever he'd taken her. She'd read something about food being provided during her MSDB experience. It was possible someone had watched Master feed her, but she hadn't sensed a presence. Most likely the cameras designed to guarantee her safety had been trained on her kneeling, bound and blindfolded body.

So why hadn't she insisted she was in the hands of a madman and wanted *out?*

Putting off having to answer her question, she concentrated on the strain on the collar. She needed to stay as close to Master as possible, because he was leading the way. Being this dependent on him increased her awareness of him even more — something she hadn't thought possible. He'd bound her wrists, secured the blindfold around her eyes and attached a leash to the collar. She was his.

So much rain ran off her it felt as if she were in a shower. There was hardly any wind and she hadn't heard thunder for a while, so maybe the storm would end before much longer.

Master stopped so abruptly she ran into him. Instead of jumping back, she soaked in his warm presence. Making her sightless way to where he'd fed her had left her with little ability to think about how he'd kept her sexually unfulfilled. Now that their bodies were touching, she could barely concentrate on anything else.

"Down on your knees again, hostage."

Hostage or slave? Which was it? Eager to please him, she did as he'd commanded. Crushed seashells bit into her knees. She placed her hands on her thighs and waited.

Because of the sound the rain made, she couldn't be sure, but she thought she heard him walking away. She kneeled with water washing over her already drenched body. The longer she waited for him, the less anything else mattered. She sank lower and lower with her head deeply bent. How naïve she'd been to think being submissive meant having a man give her a choice between a switch and a whip once she'd assured him she wanted to be lashed. Now she understood how deeply satisfying — yes, satisfying — turning her body over to a man could be. He wanted her to crouch surrounded by nature so she would.

"They aren't coming for you," he said at length. She thought he was standing behind her but couldn't be sure. "Your warriors don't dare take the chance to try to rescue you. You aren't worth risking their lives."

"I know," she whispered. She meant it. "I don't want them to."

"You're mine for as long as I want you. I'll teach you what it takes to please me and if you do, I might reward you."

"Thank you, Master."

"'Might', I said. And if I decide not to, there's nothing you can do about it."

The thought of living forever without sexual pleasure made her tremble, but he was right.

"I beg you to treat me with consideration," she said. "I'll dedicate my life to giving you pleasure. All I ask is a little —"

"I know what you need, slave."

So she was a slave again. Trying to keep up with his mental changes was so confusing — and exciting. She no longer tried to make sense of what had happened to him. What mattered was that they were together.

She swallowed. "I loved it when you pleasured me with your fingers. I felt worthy of you."

"What about when I placed clamps on your breasts and whipped you? How did that make you feel?"

"Alive," she breathed. "Newborn."

"Not afraid?"

"A little. But it was exciting."

"I could leave you out here. Secure you to a tree with your arms over your head so you can't free yourself or remove the blindfold. I might make you spend the night here so you'll comprehend what belonging to me means."

Belonging to him. She shivered and pressed her hands over her heart. Unable to think of anything to say, she waited with darkness all around her.

"But I won't, because I have other uses for you."

Chapter Twenty-One

By the time Master had finished drying her, she was half crazy from wondering what he intended to do next. Part of her questioned why she was so willing to join him in what might be his madness, but mostly she just wanted to experience. The whole time she'd watched him towel his unabashedly naked body, she'd ached to take over. She hadn't, because he hadn't given her permission.

Being able to see and use her hands again felt strange, and she wished she was still totally dependent on him. Maybe if she begged him to —

No, she wouldn't do that, because waiting for him to make the next move meant more. She wondered what their relationship as Master and slave would be like. Her career was too important to give up, but maybe he'd dictate everything about her life when she wasn't working. He'd call her during the day with a list of commands, everything from not wearing underwear to masturbating in her truck with her workmen about. Maybe he'd place a vibrator inside her before she left in the morning and warn her of the consequences if she climaxed.

Sweat broke out. Fingers clenched, she swallowed repeatedly at the thought of coming home to find Master waiting for her with his cock exposed. Trembling, she'd sink to her knees and crawl over to him. She'd take his erection into her mouth and slowly demonstrate how grateful she was for his mastery of her.

"I think — the rain is letting up."

He sounded both confused and disappointed, giving rise, once more, to the question of how much of an impact the weather had on him. If the storm – and maybe the island – was responsible for how he'd been acting, she didn't want anything to change.

Had to hold onto this strange connection to him.

She extended her hand toward his cock. "Please let me."

"You want to fuck?"

"If that's what you want," she hurried to say. "I was thinking –" She drew a less than steady hand over her mouth. "I would love to –"

"You don't make the decisions, I do."

"I know. I wasn't –"

"Be quiet." He grabbed her hair and hauled her over to the bed with the collection of bondage equipment on it. "You need to truly learn what it means to be a submissive."

Did he no longer see her as a captive or hostage? Maybe he'd broken free from the *world* that had sucked him in. She wasn't sure how she felt about that. In some respects she was relieved, because she couldn't wrap her mind around what had happened to him or how deep he might sink into that world. Besides, if he'd returned to reality, he could play the role of Dom with her as his sub.

Not a game, please.

He bent her over the side of the bed so her forehead rested on the mattress with her ass high, and left her like that as he rummaged through the various items. Finally, he picked up some white rope and made a loop at one end. He slid the loop over her arm closest to him then snagged her other arm and placed the rope around it as well. He pushed the loop up her arms until it settled just above her elbows and tightened it, drawing her arms together behind her back. Her shoulder blades burned. She felt more rope joining what was already there like a sleeve. When he'd trapped her arms in four or five loops, he ran more rope around the restraint between her elbows and tightened it. Some three or four feet of loose rope lay on her back.

"A handle." He pulled up on the excess rope. "Or reins. Regardless of what we call it, controlling you is going to be easy."

Instead of bringing her upright, he kept her dangling over the bed. She lacked the necessary leverage needed to straighten—although maybe the truth was she didn't dare do anything he hadn't given her permission to. As a result, she sagged in his grip.

"Harnessing a slave as I've done makes controlling her a simple matter." He jerked on the rope, bringing her up a few inches, then slackened his hold so she sagged again. She loved, absolutely loved, being under his control. "This approach also ensures I'll have your full attention."

"You do, Master, you do." Moisture pooled in her pussy. Only this moment mattered. There was nothing else.

"I know."

Those were the words of a sane man, not someone lost in something beyond comprehension. A little disappointed, she silently begged him to take things to the next step. He'd introduced her to what it meant to be helpless and more than a little about pain. Along with both of those experiences, there'd been a healthy dose of stimulation, complete with several climaxes.

What they hadn't done was have sex, fuck.

If he wanted to, it would happen. Otherwise, she had no choice but to accept his decision—for now.

"Master?" she ventured. "May I ask a question?"

"Ask. I may or may not answer."

Vowing to keep the questions manageable, she wrestled her thoughts into some kind of whole. "Will we see each other after this? If it's what we want, can it happen?"

He rubbed her left flank. "You want?"

Half crazed from the overload of sensation, she lifted her head, trying to read his expression, but he was behind her. "I, ah, I think so."

"I don't."

* * * *

Even though several minutes had passed since his harsh statement, she still couldn't get past it. She was nothing but a paycheck to him. Even if he comprehended how much she'd changed today, her journey didn't matter to him. She might as well be an animal he'd agreed to help train.

Too bad she didn't feel the same way.

He'd finally helped her stand upright. Then he'd ordered her to go back into the bathroom. As she stood before the mirror with him stony-faced behind her, she wondered who the stranger staring back at her was. Her minimal makeup was gone, her hair a still-damp disaster. More telling, her eyes were huge and hot, her out-thrusting nipples hard.

"Never forget what you're seeing," he ordered. "Remember the day you turned yourself over to a stranger."

"One day?" She tried to meet his gaze in the mirror.

He seemed to be staring at something only he could see. "You don't want me. Right now" — giving her no warning, he ran a hand between her legs from behind, his fingers sliding over her juice-slickened labia — "you might believe there's something between us, something worth exploring, but this is what's fueling those thoughts." He swiped again. "Don't think with your pussy because it lies."

"Don't tell me what to think," she snapped and whirled on him. Lost the intimate contact. Her edict might have had more impact if she hadn't been helpless and naked. "You don't know what's going on with me."

To her surprise, he nodded. He placed his fingers in his mouth and sucked on her fluids. "I know some things," he told her as he held up his hand, "but not everything. What I do understand is that, underneath your tough exterior, you crave having a man telling you what to do, even what to feel."

Was that true? She couldn't argue the first part of his comment, but the thought that a man could control her emotions made her shiver. She wanted back use of her arms, her clothes, wanted the collar around her neck gone.

Didn't she?

"Confused, slave?" he taunted. He hooked a finger through the ring under her chin and pulled her out of the bathroom. Her fingers fluttered uselessly. "Someday, a dominant man is going to see beneath your barriers to the real you. He'll place his collar around you and you'll kneel before him. Worship him. Find joy in the act of surrender."

She didn't want just any dominant man, she admitted, as he returned her to the bed and again bent her over it. She wanted this complex one. She was just afraid of telling him so.

"We've been through a lot," he said from his station behind and above her. "You, mostly, but me as well. Now, unless you beg me not to, I'm going to get my reward."

Chapter Twenty-Two

He'd been drunk for a long time but now he was starting to sober up. If he turned his head fast, dizziness half-blinded him, and thinking took too much effort. He felt better now that the wind no longer rattled the windows. At the same time, he could hardly wait for the next storm to hit, because it made him feel more alive than he'd ever been.

So did the slight young woman at his command. Under his domination.

He vaguely recalled calling her a hostage, a prisoner, a slave, but that might have been his imagination. What he did know was she wanted this as much as he did.

Glorying in his domination over the beautiful creature wearing his ropes, he stroked her buttocks and thighs. She sighed repeatedly and kept trying to lift her head off the bed. Doing so took strength she should've hoarded for other things and, after several attempts, she stood bent over with her arms caught behind her and her ass high, waiting for her Master.

Yes, Master. In charge of every inch of that delicious flesh.

He picked up a rubber flogger and repeatedly struck her buttocks with it. She sighed, the sounds full of surrender and pleasure. Every time he heard it, every time the flogger landed, his strength grew. This was what he'd been born for.

Maybe not born, he admitted, as he continued to condition her for the next act, but somehow in the process of becoming a man, he'd recalled that being a Dominant was deeply ingrained in him. It might have started with teenage fantasies about keeping girlfriends under lock and key, but maybe the need to control, contain and rule hadn't begun until later.

Until the island and the frequent storms that battered it had pulled him under their spells.

He put down the flogger and unceremoniously ran two fingers all the way into his slave's opening. She was so damned wet, a sopping mass of need. He could take her now, wanted to bury himself in her, or he could take things another step.

Change her even more.

He reached for a crop, spun it around in his hand and eased the handle into his slave's opening.

She felt something artificial enter her. Too far gone to try to figure out what it was, she moaned. Not long ago she'd wanted to lift her head, but being beaten had taught her to let Master have his way.

Now, she clenched her teeth and tried to breathe while whatever Master had chosen to plunder her with slipped in deeper. She stepped outside herself and mentally joined Master, *watched* as a handle attached to strips of leather disappeared inside her channel. The handle spread her, trapping her. She whimpered. Slipped deep into nerves and need.

"Take it," Master commanded. "Keep it in you."

She could do that, could please Master.

The more the foreign object invaded, the more she embraced it. Because Master wanted this thing inside her, she'd do everything possible to obey. To please him.

To give herself to him.

"I offer my body to you," she said. "You've taken me from the existence I thought I wanted, separated me from my past and made the future unimportant." She hadn't known she was going to reveal so much but now she'd started, she committed herself to continuing. "Only you and the present matter."

He didn't respond with words, but she told herself that

his hands, gentle on her spine, said he understood. Between the hard invasion in her pussy and Master's finger gliding over her, she drifted in the moment. Her body had never been in this space, never known such contentment. Yes, she craved Master's cock inside her, but his complete focus was on her, something she'd never experienced.

"My body is all I have to give you," she whispered. "Please take it as the ultimate gift it is."

"Your body isn't enough." He took hold of her hair and lifted and turned her head so they looked at each other. "Think about what you just said and ask yourself if there's more."

As he released her hair, she couldn't wrap her mind around what else he wanted from her — or maybe the truth was she needed more time to decide whether to make the ultimate sacrifice. Tears burned her eyes. She would have given a great deal to be able to wrap her arms around Master, but he wanted her bent over the bed with her arms roped.

Under his domination.

"My soul." She waited out the echo of her admission. "My heart. Those things belong to you as well."

He raked his fingers over her shoulder blades. "You're giving them to a stranger?"

Mewling like a homeless cat, she arched her spine. Gravity soon had her collapsing on the bed again. "I'm certain, Master."

"You're a fool."

Maybe. "I trust you."

"How can you, when I don't trust myself?"

That, in part, was what made being around him a magical experience. She'd always dated responsible and predictable men, men whose goals paralleled hers. Maybe that's why she'd never fallen totally in love — she'd needed something more.

Someone deeper.

"I accept you as my Master. What more do you want?"

His nails made a long, slow journey down her spine, prompting more animal sounds from her. When he reached her tailbone, he drew her ass cheeks apart, and she knew he was looking at her anus and what he'd plugged her pussy with. She took this as proof that he was acknowledging the gift of her body.

Working slowly, he drew the whip handle out of her. "It's a toy," he said. "Not designed to inflict true pain."

"I know."

"But I can use something else. Is that what you want?"

Sharp sensation. Jerking and whimpering. Helpless. "I want." She waited a moment as the impact of her admission sank in. "But that isn't all. I need — Master, I need you fucking me."

"Yeah," he muttered. "Yeah."

* * * *

He'd transferred the rope from her elbows to her wrists, keeping her arms behind her. After helping her stand upright, he'd removed the leash and reapplied the blindfold. Before robbing her of sight, he'd held up a slim but stiff, cane and another whip similar to the one he'd been teasing her with, only sturdier.

"You need pain," he said, "to increase the connection between us. But for that connection to become complete, you also need to experience helpless dependence. You think you've been there, but you're just getting started. Time for me to demonstrate."

A line of fire flamed over her right thigh.

"Master!" she gasped.

"No games this time. This is your ultimate lesson. Proof of the meaning of submission. By the time we're done you'll know whether it's what you want."

The cane struck her thigh a second time, then a third. Any thought that she could stand still while he punished the body he owned fled. She tried to back away. He whipped her left thigh.

"Master! It hurts."

"Sink into the pain. Learn from it."

He began striking her everywhere, never the same place twice in a row. Head down and arms straining, she turned this way and that. The dark world held her in its grasp and she became disoriented. Several times she cried out, but when he remained silent, she made the insane decision to match him.

She lurched forward in response to a slash on the backs of both thighs, struck a wall and turned half around. Too late she remembered she still couldn't see. As she pressed her spine against the wall, he peppered her breasts. In a way it felt good, part of her total awareness of herself. Then her breasts became too sensitive, compelling her to push off the wall. She thought she might collide with him, but he obviously had no trouble staying out of her reach.

"Is this what you want?" He switched her buttocks. "Lessons in surrender?"

She could say no. He'd stop attacking if she did.

But she would have failed both of them.

"Lessons," she said around her screaming body. "Master taking me."

He walked her around the room by repeatedly striking her ass. When she couldn't take any more of the targeted attack and tried to run, he grabbed her arm and stopped her. She spun around, hoping to keep her back from him, but that left her breasts and belly open to punishment.

Hurting. Alive. Responsive.

His. Always his.

"Ten minutes," he said after what seemed forever. "That's how long we've been at this. Say the word and it'll end."

But if I do, will it be an admission of failure?

"More," she got out.

"Damn you."

Before she could make sense of why he'd said that, he started switching her again. Her legs had a will of their own, marching her here and there, taking her to a wall, the bed, bumping into the restraint chair, carrying her back out into the middle of nothing. Master followed her everywhere, flogging her inflamed body. She was growing tired and wanted to fall down. At the same time, she didn't want to lose the most intense experience of her life. She'd survive, grow, make Master proud of her.

Make him love her.

The thought rocked her and she stood on trembling legs with her head tilted to the side. If only she could see his expression, look for the smallest sign of love in his eyes.

"Enough?" he asked.

"I...don't know."

"Then I'm making the decision."

Chapter Twenty-Three

Something clattered to the floor, telling her he no longer held what he'd been using on her. The longer the silence lasted, the more aware she became of the distance between them — a distance she didn't want.

Trusting her senses to tell her where he stood, she started toward him. Her body was still on fire, alive. Real.

When her shoulder brushed male flesh, she turned toward the contact and leaned into him. His arms went around her. Trembling, she pressed her lips against his chest. Every inch of her was electrified and so sensitive she wasn't sure she could stand to be touched.

"So brave," he muttered. "A true submissive."

The compliment, coupled with the taste of him, broke her. Whimpering, she slumped onto her knees. He caressed the top of her head. Much as the gesture meant, it wasn't enough. She wasn't his pet. Not even being his submissive slave was enough. He'd beaten her. She'd let him.

After taking a moment to gather her strength, she lifted her head and went in search of his cock. It didn't take long.

"Master," she whispered. "Please let me show my gratitude."

He groaned. "Do it."

His response left her with no doubt of the risk he was taking. It was one thing for a dominant man to exercise his control over his submissive, quite another to trust his cock to her. Would his response have been different if she hadn't told him he owned her heart and soul as well as her body?

Putting off facing the ramifications of that admission, she opened her mouth. Her flesh still throbbed. She started by leaning toward but not closing her lips around the gift he'd given her. This powerful man had altered her existence. He'd taken her into his world. Turned her into a captive, hostage, slave.

On the tail of another groan, he fisted her hair. Accepting that he could stop her at any time, she began sucking. Using her lips to clamp onto him, she leaned back. His hold on her hair remained steady — unlike his now-ragged breathing.

Not being able see him fueled her imagination. She pictured the two of them deep in the jungle his clan called home. She'd spent the day tethered by the neck to his shelter but, at last, he'd returned. Other male clan members were with him, staring at but not touching what belonged to Master.

The warriors had eaten and he'd fed her a few scraps. Only then had he untied her and hauled her to where he slept.

"Present," he ordered.

Afraid and compliant, she positioned herself on her hands and knees with her buttocks close to his cock. Maybe he'd fuck her. Maybe he'd ream her in the ass. Whichever he chose, she'd accept.

Only she wasn't on her hands and knees, she reminded herself, as reality returned. They were in a bedroom. Her hands were still behind her, she wore his blindfold and her body still hurt, proof of her place in his world.

Master took as his due that she'd administer to his cock, so that was what she did. Concentrating on giving him maximum pleasure and ignoring her needs was impossible, but she fought to make him her priority.

She felt connected to him, part and parcel of the man. Eyes closed behind the blindfold, she worshiped him with tongue and lips. That coupled with his uneven breathing fueled a fire the beating she'd *endured* had started. She moved him about, took him deep, withdrew, turned her head to the side so his tip pushed against the inside of her cheek.

This flesh, muscle and blood became her god.

"Enough," he said.

He pulled her head back until she had no choice but to let him go. Despite his fingers in her hair, she tried to recapture his cock.

"Not like that." He pressed the flat of his hand against her lips. "There are limits to what I can…"

What he hadn't said but she suspected was that he'd nearly come in her mouth. A small measure of power rested beside the reality of her bondage. She continued her blind search for him.

"What is this about?" He grabbed her chin, immobilizing her. "Didn't you hear what I said?"

"I heard, Master, but I need…"

"Need what?"

"You," she whispered.

"Do you?" he asked following a telling silence. "What about a shower and some salve?"

His attempt to remind her of what her body had been through barely made an impact. She craved the feel of him in her mouth.

"Don't." He forced her head up, grabbed a nipple and tightened his hold. "What the hell's wrong with you?"

"Nothing." Didn't he understand how right everything could be if he'd just let her wrap her body around his? She'd stretch out on the bed, open her legs and draw him into her. They'd go from being two to one.

Unite.

"Nothing?" he repeated. He let go of her chin, captured her other nipple and drew her onto her feet. "What's going on with my horny little slave?"

Slave. Captive. Hostage. All the same. "You left me alone too long, Master," she told him. "You were gone all day. I was afraid maybe you'd been injured in battle, maybe even killed. If you didn't return, I'd…"

"What if I didn't return?" he prompted, with his fingers still strong on her nipples. "Where were you?"

"In the jungle." Surely he knew that. "Tied to your shelter."

"Tell me about it."

She took a deep breath that smelled of a wet, wild world and him. "You'd captured me in a raid. For days you dragged me behind you as you and the rest of your clan went deep into the jungle. Then you chose a spot to stay while you hunted. You burned my clothes, roped me to a tree. Before you left, you told me to prepare myself because when you returned you were going to turn me into your sex slave."

"How did you feel about that?"

The ache in her breasts had all but disappeared while she was spinning her tale. "Afraid. Excited. I knew—from the moment you knocked me to the ground, I knew what my fate was going to be."

"And that excited you?"

"Yes," she admitted with darkness all around. "Yes."

"Because?"

"Because I wanted to belong to you."

When he untied her arms, she stood with them dangling at her sides. He wasn't sure she realized she could remove her blindfold. The switch had left long, thin red marks all over her body but hadn't broken any flesh. They'd fade in a few days. At least the surface proof of what she'd gone through would end. As for the deeper impact—

Watching the slender, vulnerable woman wait for his next move, he recalled bits and pieces of what he'd done, said and thought since the storm struck. He'd experienced similar things here before, which was why he'd been hesitant to return to the island. He had because, as unnerving as imagining himself to be a primitive warrior had been, he'd never felt more alive. In the past, he'd managed to distance himself from the woman he'd been paired with before all hell had broken loose.

This time, with this one, he hadn't tried.

Why me?

When she sighed and cocked her head, he knew she still envisioned herself as a naked captive and future sex slave.

The storm, island, or maybe both, had captured her as thoroughly as it had him.

Not understanding how that had happened, he pulled the blindfold off her. She rubbed her eyes then lightly fingered her breasts.

"Study yourself, slave," he ordered. "See what your Master has done to you."

Mouth open, she did as he'd commanded. He studied her every move while she traced the marks. She didn't wince as she caressed what he'd done to her.

"Do you understand what they represent?" he asked.

She licked a forefinger and rubbed the moisture over her nipples. "My Master has marked me. Left proof that I belong to you."

"How do those marks make you feel?"

For the first time following being given back the right to see, she looked up at him. Her eyes had darkened so they reminded him of midnight.

"Owned," she whispered. "Worthy of Master."

It had happened. She'd entered the place he'd long believed only he inhabited.

"Express your gratitude, then."

She stared at his erection. "What do you want of me?"

Chapter Twenty-Four

"Look into yourself and do what feels right."

Master's words swirled around her. She left him and walked over to the window so she could breathe in some of the air that meant so much to him. The rain had practically stopped but the wind had increased. It had also cooled off a little, drawing her attention to the deepening shadows. It would soon be dark.

Feeling renewed, she faced him. Seeing him looking like a primitive lord heated her. She smiled then tried to recall whether this was the first time she'd done so today.

'Look into yourself and do what feels right'. Would a Master say that to a slave?

She tried to remind herself that she wasn't his possession, only to lose the thought. Today their worlds didn't go any farther than this room. Tomorrow didn't exist.

"I want to make love with you," she whispered.

"*With* me?"

His voice didn't sound any stronger than hers had. He appeared shocked.

"Yes." She could barely believe she'd said what she had.

"As Shana or a captive?"

He hadn't spoken her name before. She would have remembered those notes if he had. "It doesn't matter."

"It will."

In the future, that place she couldn't envision. "I don't know how to do this," she admitted. She felt not virgin-shy but new. As she waited to see if the feeling would change, she fingered the marks on her belly. Maybe she'd stay naked for as long as they lasted.

"Then come with me," he said.

She started to walk toward him but stopped when he shook his head.

"Come in your mind." He pointed at the bed. "You're at the camp where your captor compelled you to stay. He has returned. He's weary, but he isn't ready to go to sleep. What happens between the two of you?"

Just like that, she slipped into the place where everything was primal. All around them other warriors were starting to snore. She'd long ago dismissed any thoughts of trying to flee, in part because she didn't know where she was — but mostly because this man had changed so much of what she'd believed about herself. He'd brought her into his basic world, not so much by force but because his body was made for physical action.

And he deserved an equal.

"We reach for each other," she told the man who'd asked the question. "I offer myself to my captor."

"Why?"

"Because he has shown me my core, forced me to be honest with myself."

"You weren't honest before?"

"I didn't know it, but I'd been denying the real me, a woman who longed to submit."

She'd said all she could. If he didn't understand, she didn't know how to reach him.

"I don't want your submission," he said.

For a moment she thought she'd lost him. Then she noted the light in his eyes and it all came together. "Fucking partners," she said.

"That's one way of putting it."

He'd told her to think of herself as a newcomer to his world, so she did just that as she climbed onto the bed. Kneeling, she fingered her collar. "This defines much of our relationship, but not all of it." Taking her time, she traced a line from her throat all the way to her crotch. She owned her body and yet she didn't. "This is the core of what exists between us." She extended glistening fingers toward his cock.

"Only that?"

Don't press me. "For now. Master, please."

Somber, he closed the space between them and planted his hands on the bed inches from her knees. They stared at each other for a long time. Finally, she placed her hands over his.

"Please, Master," she whispered.

He climbed onto the bed and pushed her onto her back. Moaning, she bent her knees and spread her legs. He entered the space she'd created and slid his hands under her buttocks. As he lifted her lower body off the bed, her heart hammered and her pussy dripped.

"My slave," he muttered. "And my equal."

Overwhelmed by what he'd thrown at her, she extended her arms toward him. Her fingers grazed his chest. Outside, the wind slammed into the side of the building with so much force that she felt the vibration throughout.

Certain she wouldn't run, her captor had freed her from the tree she'd spent the day tethered to. He'd sat by a warming fire with the rest of his clan's braves as they'd discussed tomorrow's plans, but she'd paid little attention to the conversation, because she'd been kneeling beside him and he'd stroked her the whole time, preparing her for the night.

Whimpering, she shook off the image and tried to sit up on the bed. Without support behind her, she had no choice but to fall back down. She kept her arms outstretched toward him.

"Master? I need — please."

Nodding, he took hold of her ankles and dragged her closer, keeping her spread as he did. His cock tip kissed her opening.

"Yes," she whimpered. "Yes."

"In all ways?"

"Yes," she repeated. "I'm yours to —"

"Only if it's right for you, too."

A primitive warrior wouldn't say that. "It is," she told the man who shared the real world with her. Master, I beg you, I need—"

Before she could finish, he pushed into her. His heat, bulk and length filled her. Crying out, she clamped her legs around him with all her strength. He began riding her, his thrusts hard and fast. She slid over the coverlet, growling like an animal.

Master was fucking her. Using her body, rewarding it, turning them from two into one. In the past, she'd felt a measure of superiority because her lovers had to enter her, but this was different. No matter that Master groaned and even cursed, he was in charge. She bucked under him, reared and whimpered, clawed at his flesh and clenched his cock with all the strength in her core.

Thrust by thrust, she lost herself. Desire raged through her, compelling her to grip his buttocks and pull him even closer. He responded by slamming into her so hard she wondered if they'd break the bed. The hours leading to this moment swirled together in her fracturing mind until she had no idea where they were.

It didn't matter. She and Master were having sex. At the same time, her captor was fucking her in the middle of the wilderness.

Electrically charged night air stroked her straining flesh. Knowing he was experiencing the same explosion filled her with wild joy. He was so drenched in sweat she had to struggle to hold on to him, but grip him she did, because he'd become her life.

Her world.

A glory of pulsing heat tore into her and she screamed. Her climax was a beast, hard and strong. Going on and on. Above and inside her, Master bellowed through his own release. Despite the haze of her existence, she shared his moments with him. Prayed he was doing the same.

Master. Owner. Giver of a reason to live.

Chapter Twenty-Five

He hadn't immediately crawled off her. During those moments when his body had trapped hers, she'd gone from exhaustion to acceptance to something she didn't understand and wasn't ready to face.

At length, he got up and walked into the bathroom, leaving her to listen to her heartbeat and the wind attacking the vegetation. He was in there so long she went from floating to asking herself if he was deliberately avoiding her.

She was a mess.

It took most of her strength to sit up. Once she had, she was sorry because she had no choice but to acknowledge her striped legs. Shaking her head in disbelief, she touched the marks on her belly. When doing that brought no answers, she did the same to her breasts. They were so sensitive she couldn't hold back a long, low hiss. After sliding over to the side of the bed so she could lower her feet to the floor, she separated her legs and hesitantly touched her pussy.

Whatever had happened between Master and her hadn't been fucking and it certainly hadn't been lovemaking. She couldn't even call it sex.

Something stirred deep inside her. She knew better than to test her resolve, but that didn't stop her from fingering her opening. In only a few seconds, her clit hardened.

Her captor had had his way with her. When he'd finished, he'd tied her to him via rope around both their wrists. He'd fallen asleep, something she knew she couldn't do.

After a long period of inactivity, she loosened the knots against her wrist. When she'd freed herself, she crawled away from him. Ahead of her lay the unknown—and a chance to regain her freedom. Behind her slept a man who believed he had every right to her body.

A man who'd already claimed it once tonight and would do so again when he wakened.

What should she do? Rely on her instinct for survival or surrender freedom?

"Are you all right?"

Jolted back to the real world by the unexpected question, she acknowledged the man she had to stop thinking of as her Master. She kept her fingers on her sex.

"No, I'm not."

"You hurt—?"

"It's not that," she snapped even though her whole body ached. "I didn't know it was going to be like this, that you'd—that I'd— Damn it, it's too much."

"Are you sorry?"

He hadn't bothered putting on clothes, which she took as an unspoken announcement that he expected to fuck her again before the night was over. Even as she railed at his arrogance, she understood why he felt that way.

"I'm a lot of things," she said as she stood. Her legs were shaky, not that she'd let him know. "Mostly, I'm a mess."

He folded his too-big arms across his too-big chest. "Are you?"

Don't let him see down to the truth. "I need a damn shower." Her fingers were wet with her arousal and his cum. "My hair's dirty. I hope there's a brush in—"

He pointed at the bathroom door. "Do what you have to."

"I intend to." Head high, shoulders back and legs trembling with what she told herself was exhaustion, she walked past him.

She closed the door behind her and reached for the light switch but didn't turn it on. She wasn't ready to see herself. It felt strange to be alone—strange in ways she didn't want to have to try to define.

Determined not to think about him, or anything, she reluctantly filled the room with light. She kept her back to the mirror while turning on the shower and selecting a washcloth and towel.

The warm, gently falling water felt glorious on her abused body. As she slowly soaped herself, she noted that every time soap touched a new place, it soothed. If she was going to get involved in the BDSM lifestyle she had to make sure she had some of that brand of soap.

If she got involved?

Did she want to go there?

Would her mind, her soul survive if she did?

Shampooing her hair and standing under the spray for a good five minutes brought her no closer to an answer. One thing she knew — the man in the next room scared the crap out of her.

* * * *

"You can't make me stay."

"That's not what I said. There's no way off the island until morning."

"What if I insist they get a boat here?"

He'd seen her naked with her pussy on display, to say nothing of burying himself in her, so what the hell was so unnerving about knowing she wore nothing under the large white towel she'd wrapped around herself? She'd made a stab at brushing her hair. Unfortunately for his nervous system, she still looked untamed. While she'd been in the bathroom, he'd turned off all lights except a small lamp. As a result, shadows played with her edges.

She scared the crap out of him.

"MSDB only works with two captains, and they don't run their boats at night." He supposed he should add that she was safe with him, but it might've been a lie.

Danger went both ways.

"What about the main building? I want to wait there."

"Do you?"

"Damn you," she muttered before walking over to the

window. The island had no outside lighting beyond the cabins, and the clouds covered the moon, which meant she was staring at darkness, the same dark he'd nearly lost himself in while she'd been in the bathroom.

"I'm not afraid of the night," she muttered. "I often go for long walks after work. Doing so relaxes me."

He wasn't sure what she was getting at, if anything. Maybe if he said nothing, she'd forget he was here and —

She was right. Things had been too damn intense between them. The storm hadn't helped. The beasts of rain, wind, thunder and lightning had both sucked him up and torn him apart. He had vague memories of doing and saying things that had probably worried her. Obviously she'd said what she had about not being afraid of the night in an attempt to reassure herself. He didn't blame her. Hell, if he thought he could say the right things, he'd apologize for putting her through what he had — whatever that was.

At least the storm had spent itself. He was free of it.

Until the next time.

"I didn't know it would be like that."

"Like what?"

She whirled on him, nearly losing the towel as she did. Her gaze flickered to the cock he hadn't bothered covering up. His blood started pumping, proof — not that he needed any — that he'd been affected by more than the island and weather. He wondered what might happen between them if they'd met in ordinary circumstances, whatever those were.

"You can't need me to spell it out," she snapped.

Her eyes said she wanted nothing to do with this conversation but her body said something different. Despite her sharp words, she carried herself as if she didn't know what to do with her form. Maybe she was waiting for him to tell her, to issue an order.

No, damn it, they weren't going down that road again.

"I thought coming here would give me the opportunity to sample the BDSM lifestyle, to see if aspects of it might appeal to me."

She sounded as if she'd wanted to take BDSM for a test drive. Maybe he should tell her it wasn't like that. At least, it hadn't been that simple for him.

"What I introduced you to didn't live up to your expectations?"

"I'm not sure what my expectations were," she whispered.

She wrapped her arms around her middle, the gesture causing her breasts to expand under the terrycloth. He'd been wise to sit down. Otherwise he might have already thrown her onto the tangled spread.

Taken them to a place neither of them wanted.

"I didn't know it was going to be so intense," she continued. "That I'd…"

"That you'd what?" he prompted. He sensed they were getting to something important.

She started to extend a hand toward him, only to hug herself again. She was so damned small and vulnerable, submissive even. That was what was tearing him apart, the passive current running beneath her kick-ass exterior.

He wanted to exploit that.

Knew it would be the death of him.

"I don't know how it happened," she said softly, "or why. But by the end of, you know, I'd stopped being Shana. I forgot all about how I could pull the plug on what was happening simply by saying the word red."

So had he.

"I'd become the captive of a nameless savage, a warrior," she continued. "I was utterly at his mercy and yet…"

She'd become? Shock slammed into him. It took all his self-control not to go to her.

She looked at the floor. "My captor had been gone a long time. I don't know what he'd been doing, maybe fighting his enemies, maybe hunting. When he returned, he took me."

"Raped you?" Saying the word made him sick to his stomach.

"No. It wasn't that because I, ah, I needed him."

It wouldn't be morning for hours. How the hell was he going to get through it with her so near, so untouchable? Damn it, he should stand near the recording device that had been placed in the overhead light and tell management to come get her.

"Once he fell asleep," she went on as he admitted he couldn't make himself do that, "I could have run away. I should have. But I didn't."

Talking must have worn her out because she stumbled back and let the wall support her. When she leaned her head against the window screen, he half expected the wilderness to reach in and spirit her away.

If it had, he would have gone after her.

"I stayed because I needed him."

"Maybe," he tried, "you'd decided he represented less of a threat than the wilderness did."

"No. I needed—I wanted him."

And for a while earlier today, he'd been that savage.

It could happen again.

"It became real to you?" he asked.

In her slow nod he read not just acceptance but a kind of peace. "I know it sounds crazy. I anticipated engaging in a few hours of role playing by coming here. I never thought I'd get so carried away."

She should see things from his perspective—except maybe she had.

"I deal with dirt, rocks and things that grow." Her attention shifted from his face to his chest and started drifting lower. "I live in the real world, not…"

"Sometimes things change," was the best he could come up with.

She shuddered and pulled the towel tighter over her breasts. "I don't like that kind of change. You might be comfortable with it, but I'll never be." She turned slightly so she could again rest her cheek against the screen and absorb the post-storm night. "That's why I can hardly wait to leave."

Even though she hadn't said it, he knew it was him she needed to separate herself from most of all.

"In the morning." Determined not to think, he pulled back the covers and slipped naked between the sheets. "Turn off the light when you're ready to come to bed. There's room for both of us."

Hadn't he given her what he believed she needed? Why was she looking as if he'd just struck her?

"Trust me." Hating what he was doing, he rolled onto his side, facing away from her. "I'm not going to touch you."

"Good," she muttered. "Good."

Chapter Twenty-Six

Warriors from several clans had come to this place by the river, because everyone was weary of fighting. An elder from each clan had presented his people's grievances. The list of wrongs done had taken most of the day but finally the discussion had turned to how important it was to put those things behind them and move forward.

Her captor had brought her to the meeting. Other tribes had done the same and there were at least a dozen hostages. The decision had already been made not to try to determine which clan had been wronged the most. Instead of arguing whether a clan should be required to pay for the return of a captive and how much the ransom or prisoner price should be, the elders had agreed they'd never be able to satisfy everyone. Fathers didn't want to be responsible for daughters who'd been passed around and thus had lost their value. It was better for them to stay where they were.

Her people had no use for her. After days and nights spent dreaming of freedom, she now understood that would never be. She and the other captives were considered soiled and worthless to the clans of their birth.

She'd spent the long day kneeling near her captor with his ropes on her wrists and his hand occasionally on her exposed breasts. She hadn't had to look up at him to understand the message he was giving out. He considered her his property.

His.

Destined to spend the rest of her life on her knees before him, except when he had other uses for her.

As several older women stepped forward to start the evening fire and begin preparations for the peace meal, she made comparisons between her future and theirs. As free women, they had countless responsibilities and tasks that, over time, would bow their backs and cripple their hands. They'd carry water long distances, build the structures their families used, gather wood and much of the foodstuffs. Their men hunted, but then they turned the game over to their women to gut, skin, cut up, smoke and cook.

As a slave, a sex slave, her life would be quite different. She anticipated being required to do many of the things the free women did, but her loads would always be lighter so she'd remain what her owner required of the female who shared his bed.

"The elders have spoken," Master said. "You will be mine for as long as we both live. Now I can mark you." He made his point by pressing his fingertips against the top of her left breast. "The tattoo will proclaim my ownership."

Her heart raced as she lifted her bound arms and placed her hands between her breasts. "I will wear it proudly," she told him. "A warrior's slave must never doubt who owns her."

Laughing, he grabbed the ropes around her wrists and hauled her to her feet. She thought he'd take her into the woods and fuck her while waiting for dinner. Even though she hadn't eaten today, anticipation made her empty belly unimportant. Master fucked well. Sometimes he prepared her in a special way that involved a switch. Occasionally he forced her to bend over a log so he could take her from behind as if she were his animal. Rarely, he ordered her to join him on his sleeping pallet. Once there, she straddled his hips, placed his cock inside her, and did all the work while he entertained himself by playing with or abusing her breasts.

She loved all his ways.

She'd even been looking forward to wearing Master's brand.

"Over my knees," he ordered.

Shaking off the secret places her mind had gone to, she stretched out with her middle resting on his thighs, her feet scraping over the ground and her head and arms hanging. He pushed her legs apart and rammed his thumb into her sex.

"Here's proof of what this captive has become," he announced to the crowd she could no longer see. "I've taught her to be my pleasure slave." He started pushing in and out, making her moan and squirm. "She didn't cry when she learned of her fate today because this is all she wants."

All. Helpless to fight her body's need for his expertise. A slave to his domination over her.

"Master, Master," she whimpered. She couldn't hold still, didn't care that they had an audience. "I — please fuck me."

Chapter Twenty-Seven

"Shana. Shana."

Desperate to stay with the dream, she slapped the hand on her shoulder.

"Sorry, but I'm not going to let you go back." He shook her again.

"Go back where?" she muttered with her eyes closed. Despite her efforts to not let it happen, the *world* she'd been living in faded.

"To where *it* wants to take you."

As Master's words made more of an impact, she acknowledged his wisdom. *It* might be all the explanation she'd ever have for why her imagination took flight. His hand continued to rest on her shoulder, as if he had every right to touch her like that.

They'd had an intense conversation before going to bed. Mostly, she'd made it clear — or tried to make it clear — that she didn't want anything more to do with MSDB and everything it represented. As a result, the man beside her wasn't her Master. He was — what?

She was what?

"You were begging someone to fuck you," he said. "You called that person 'Master'. Do you know who it was?"

You, and you know it. "Sorry." Hating the evasion, she bought time by getting out of bed and turning on the lamp. The covers ended at his waist, leaving his chest in glorious view and drawing her thoughts to what was hidden. "You, ah, know how dreams are. Pretty hard to nail down."

He sat up and slid over to the side of the bed, leaving the covers behind.

Damn him for having an erection.

Damn him for being so male.

"Come back to bed," he said. "I won't touch you."

She wasn't sure she could make the same promise, but standing here shivering when her body felt as if she'd been in a wrestling match didn't make much sense. She slipped around him and sat cross-legged behind him. His back became her world.

"I have dreams," he said, without turning toward her. "Vivid ones that hit me most nights. They're basically the same and— I don't remember a lot of what I did or said to you, but have no doubt that today ran parallel to what takes over when I'm asleep." He let out a long, low breath. "It's one thing to be in the grip of something inescapable when I'm alone in bed, quite another when it's daytime and a storm…"

Storm.

Struggling with herself, she gently fingered the nipples he'd clamped earlier. Something about the gesture made up her mind for her.

"I was part of some primitive society," she told him. "The rules were different from what I'm used to, a kind of 'to the victor go the spoils' mentality."

"And you were a spoil."

"Yeah." Strengthened by thoughts of what his broad back and powerful shoulders were capable of, she detailed everything she could remember about what had been deeper than a dream. She made no judgments about her behavior or that of her captor. Certain things had simply happened.

"I accepted my fate," she said at length. "Worshiped it."

"I know."

Instead of being shocked, she nodded at his back. "Tell me about your dreams."

Now it was his turn to get up and position himself by the window. It was still humid and hot, the aftermath of a Florida summer storm. Despite the now-still air, she felt invigorated.

Turned on.

"As a warrior, it's my responsibility to protect my clan. I risk my life to assure theirs." He placed his hands on the screen. "From childhood I accepted my role. Warriors don't speak of fear. If I don't acknowledge my vulnerability, it doesn't exist."

"It does exist," she whispered. "You're human."

"Am I? Sometimes I wonder."

Frightened for him, she got out of bed and joined him. Most of the clouds had dissipated while she'd been asleep. The nearly full moon illuminated the thick vegetation and brought home the message of how isolated they were. Much as she needed to touch him, she didn't.

"Do you ever wish you weren't a warrior?" she asked. "Maybe you'd like other responsibilities."

He shook his head. "In my day job, I'm a lawyer. I don't know if I told you that. My life — much of my life — is defined by the law. I can't always prosecute those who deserve to be and sometimes my job calls for putting away someone who never had a chance. I'm expected to see life as black and white and follow the law, but it isn't that simple."

She'd given thought to how the legal system worked, but never like this.

"There's no getting away from it — until something I don't comprehend and can't stop turns me into someone who lives or dies by the strength in his arm and sharpness of his knife."

"A man who needs to control," she said. "And knows how to make it happen."

"Yeah." He ended his study of the world beyond those walls and stared down at her. Made her feel small. "MSDB gives me a structure for taking control, but it isn't always enough."

She couldn't think what had happened to her clothes or why she needed to be naked before him. "Storms change things for you." She felt wise. "They allow you to break free of constraint and convention, to enter another realm."

He fingered her collar. "The same happens to you."

"Yes," she admitted as her pussy flooded.

"Maybe one rainy day I'll come to where you're working. It'll be nearly dark." His voice dropped to a whisper. "You won't know I'm there as you walk around the worksite making sure your employees didn't leave any tools out. You've sent them home and are looking forward to getting out of the rain. You're wearing a hooded raincoat. Your view of your surroundings is compromised. You walk around the back of your equipment trailer where there's little light."

She'd been in situations like that, the last to leave, the one working alone as night had pressed around her. Most times she was too focused on her task to think about her isolation, but occasionally she'd wished she'd been carrying mace.

"Suddenly someone grabs you. He clamps a hand over your mouth. You can't scream. He lifts you off your feet with your arms pinned to your sides and carries you to his van. He throws you inside and…"

She couldn't hear the rest of what he was saying for the sound of her blood roaring in her ears. The dark stranger could be a mugger, a thief intent on stealing her tools. Or he might want to lock her inside his vehicle and take her somewhere even more isolated where he'd rape and eventually kill her.

That man wasn't Master. Neither was he the warrior, captor or savage of her erotic imaginings.

Instead he was a monster.

A nightmare.

"Don't." She pushed his hand away. "I don't want to do this anymore."

He leaned toward her. "I think you do."

Everything about the past few hours had been beyond her control, her fantasies most of all. "How can you say that when you don't understand what's happening to you? Not once during the — During what took place did you remind me that I could say red if things became too intense."

His features seemed to sag. "I didn't think—"

"No, you didn't. If you had you would have realized how overwhelmed I was." She hated herself for blaming him for her emotions but couldn't stop. "You sucked me so deep into your delusions that they became mine. I left this world"—she jabbed a finger at their surroundings—"and entered yours. That's insane!"

"You enjoyed most of what happened."

"Of course I did," she said. Her anger was already subsiding. What she couldn't put behind her was the depth of his impact on her—her loss of self-control. "I'm a red-blooded female and you're good at arousing one."

His nod reached her deeper than she wanted to be reached. It was all too much.

"Think about it." She slipped a finger under the collar. "There's nothing normal about our relationship."

"I never said there was."

"Didn't you?" she threw at him. "You think you can just seek me out some day when you have the time? Most men would call first, maybe ask if I'd like to go out for a drink or dinner. They wouldn't think to scare the shit out of me by jumping me and—"

"Yeah." His arms hung at his sides. "I'm not most men." He looked out of the window. "I'm lost."

Don't do this! I don't want to care about you.

Everything had gone sideways between them. That said, she still craved the feel, the taste, the sound of him. Maybe she always would.

But what they had going wasn't safe or sane. The next time it stormed he'd turn into a Dom, a Master in search of a slave. He wouldn't be interested in role playing and he sure as hell wouldn't concern himself with her willingness.

Whether it happened tomorrow or next week, eventually it would start raining and he'd come for her. He'd gag her, throw her into his vehicle and take her—take her—

"There has to be a flashlight here. Give it to me. I'll find my way to the dock. Wait there for the morning boat."

"Shana, no."

Her name on his tongue again. Tearing her apart. Making her ache to get to know who he was on sunlit days off the island.

"Yes." Her hands shook as she searched the collar for the clasp. Feeling numb and sick, she drew it off her neck. She refused to ask herself why she hadn't done this before.

"I'll go," he said. "You stay here."

He was offering to step into the night? Maybe putting himself at risk for something she might never comprehend?

"I need to be outside," she heard herself say. She tried to hand him the collar. When he didn't take it, she dropped it. "To walk and think—safe in the knowledge that you aren't around."

He studied the discarded proof of her subservience. "You don't trust me."

I don't trust myself around you. I'm not sure I ever will. "That's right," she lied.

Chapter Twenty-Eight

She should've asked the powers that be at MSDB what kind of flashlight the one she held was, because it was the strongest she'd ever seen. It not only showed her where she was walking, it illuminated the vegetation ahead of her for several hundred feet. Unfortunately, it remained dark behind her.

Foolish, she berated herself. *Stupid.*

And a coward, don't forget that.

With every step she questioned her sanity. It made absolutely no sense for her to be out in the middle of the night when there was a perfectly good bed in the cabin, to say nothing of no bugs or critters inside the four walls.

Master was there.

Stop thinking of him like that! she continued her inner lecture. The Master-sub experiment was over. She'd broken free of whatever madness had engulfed her. She couldn't do anything to wrench him loose, not that she suspected he wanted a vanilla life.

Her breathing quickened as she recalled how he'd looked standing under the porch light while she'd descended the stairs. She'd put on her sandals and wrapped another large towel around herself before taking off. In contrast, as far as she knew, he was still naked.

Walk. Just walk.

As soon as someone showed up at the dock she'd insist on getting back her belongings. She wouldn't say more than what was absolutely necessary while waiting to be taken back to the mainland, and no way would she fill out some stupid evaluation form.

MSDB was behind her.

Master was part of yesterday — if it was past midnight.

A shiver slid down her spine at the thought that he might be stalking her. Considering what he'd said about surprising her at work, she'd be wise not to put anything past him.

Hell, maybe he'd grab her here. Take her to his hideout. Keep her.

* * * *

Rope around her neck. More fibers squeezing her elbows together behind her. Another length hobbling her and causing her to stumble as she fought to keep up with the big naked man hauling her into the night.

Ferns and leaves brushed her bare flesh. She couldn't see because he'd put a blindfold over her eyes. He'd also gagged her, not that it mattered.

Every step she took caused the cotton strands against her labia to stimulate her. She'd fought him as he'd snugged the rope around her waist and had drawn it between her legs, but had stopped resisting once the impact of what he'd done registered. Every move sent more fire to her core.

Fire that made her feel alive.

He'd told her he lived deep in the forest where his enemies couldn't find him — where he'd be free to take her at all times and in all ways. The last thing he'd said before they'd struck out had been that she'd be more than ready for his cock by the time they reached their destination.

He was right. She was high with need, hot with desire. So terribly hungry for her captor.

Her Master.

* * * *

She sat slumped back on the wooden bench on the dock as the horizon started to lighten. Although she couldn't be sure, she figured she'd been here for at least three hours, sometimes dozing but mostly sitting and thinking.

Thinking about walking blind and mute into a wild world while controlled by a nameless and powerful man.

She chalked the experience up to a combination of exhaustion plus constant sexual stimulation and submission training, and told herself the journey into the wilderness had been nothing more than her imagination. And when she felt tension against her sex she told herself she'd stop having those thoughts, that sensation, once she'd gotten some sleep.

Gotten away from this damned island.

Trying to keep the towel on when there was no one to see her seemed foolish so she'd left it to its own devices as she'd tried to nap. As a result, it had slid off her breasts and lay puddled on her lap and the bench.

Hoping to hurry the day, she kept staring at the slowly brightening sky while straining to hear something other than waves and seabirds. The breeze seemed to be picking up.

Why hadn't she asked Master what time the boat would arrive?

Why hadn't she insisted on getting something to eat before coming here?

Why not a lot of things?

The eastern sunrise was more muted than on most mornings, but she refused to acknowledge that the clouds were responsible. Before long today's weather wouldn't matter to her.

It would to Master.

"Stop it!"

If she had a decent brain cell she'd stand up and pace. Instead, she brushed the towel off her lap and eased her fingers over her so-sensitive pussy. As dark as it still was, she couldn't tell whether her pussy was as red as it felt. Earlier, she'd explored to see if her skin still carried the marks Master had put on her. She'd encountered nothing but smooth flesh. Would she have nothing to remember him by?

As if in reaction to the stupid question, her inner muscles tightened. Wondering if she could fool herself into believing Master's fingers were responsible, she slipped her forefinger into her wet opening. Her head fell back and she slouched forward on the wooden seat. She didn't rush the invasion. Instead, she worked up an image of Master standing over her while she was spread out on the bed. This time no ropes or chains held her in place. She was there of her own free will.

"A well-trained slave," Master said. *"I'm proud of you."*

She closed her eyes to hold the morning at bay and so she could expand on what she was experiencing. Master was smiling down at her, with a gentle yet all-powerful expression that touched every part of her.

She was what he wanted her to be, his loving submissive.

Loving?

Groaning, she sat upright and reluctantly deserted her pussy. She had to clasp her hands to keep them off herself. Opening her eyes didn't do enough to return her to what had always been the real world.

She was losing it. The boat couldn't get here fast enough. Putting the pieces of her back together wouldn't be such a huge task if the weather would cooperate. Why the hell did it have to look as if might start storming again?

Glancing overhead, she noted that the clouds were still a distance away but, unless the now sharp wind died before much longer, she'd have to search for cover.

Did the boats run in weather like today threatened to be?

What was Master doing? Had the wind reached him? Maybe he was looking out of the window or standing on the porch waiting for the first raindrop?

More importantly, did he dread or embrace the approaching storm?

"You don't want to stay out here."

Chapter Twenty-Nine

Shock brought her to her feet. She grabbed the towel but couldn't think how to cover herself.

"What are you doing here?" she asked the man she might always think of as Master. "I told you—"

"I checked the weather report. There's going to be a lot of lightning. The boat captains refuse to be out in it."

Trapped. No way off the island until nature had had its way.

Master was at least a hundred feet away, standing at the end of the path with trees, vines and ground cover around him. He wore nothing. Didn't seem to care.

He ran his hand over his chest. "I can feel it."

"The storm's power." It wasn't a question.

"Yes." He closed then opened his eyes.

From this distance, she could only surmise that they were black.

"I couldn't stop myself from coming after you," he said. "I can fight—I *will* fight the force, but if you want to be safe, you need to go to the main building. I'll show you the way."

The main building offered food and probably her belongings. She might hook up with the two women she'd come to the island with. She'd probably run into one of MSDB's staff members. Not only would they cater to her until the weather changed, she could tell them all about the crazy man who'd—who'd…

His shelter had been created from sturdy branches and large leaves. From a distance, it was indistinguishable from its surroundings, but up close the workmanship showed. This was a primitive structure made from what was at hand, but it would withstand anything short of a hurricane.

Master led her into it then removed her gag. He let go of the leash and stepped back. Obviously, he wanted her to take in what he'd created.

This wasn't just her prison. It could become her home. Where she might spend the rest of her life.

"Incredible," she told him.

"What about this?" He pointed at the back of the building.

Even though she needed to continue to study his naked strength, she turned toward where he'd directed. The bed was large enough for two, made from a network of branches with thick vegetation over that, and topped with animal skins. An ornate storage box had been placed nearby. It was open so she could see more rope like what held her, several whips and at least two hand-carved dildos.

"For my slave," he said. "To mark our relationship."

"Shana? Did you hear me?"

They'd played out this scenario or one like it before, so she should know she was being pulled between reality and something else. This time, she didn't push away the images of what her life would be like as Master's submissive property. Instead, she let the two worlds stand side by side.

"I hear you," she told him as she started toward him. She left the towel behind, felt the wind on her skin and in her hair. "The question is, can you hear me?"

"I'm trying." He faced into the wind. "I am who I am. I have a job I both love and hate. Sometimes it consumes me and I'm relatively safe from the — the other." He raked his fingers through his wild hair. "Then I let my guard down and — you see what happens."

"Let your guard down?" she whispered. Her legs were getting weaker by the second. She could barely hear herself speak for the roaring in her head. A blink and her captor's wilderness shelter replaced the path. "Don't you mean you embrace what you're capable of? What brings you joy?"

"Call it what you want to." He threw back his shoulders so he stood straighter and widened his stance. His cock had been flaccid when she'd first seen him. It now stood as a hard testament to his masculinity, challenging and promising. "We're going to get wet."

She didn't care and was desperate to let him know. Everything except him went out of focus as she sank to her knees before him and used his hips and thighs to help her keep her balance.

"Master," she whispered. "I was wrong to think I could or should leave." His cock was so close, but he hadn't given her permission to touch it. "I can't always be with you. Like you I have...responsibilities. But if you'll have me —"

He grabbed her hair. "You're submitting?"

Surrender. Live. "Yes, Master. My place is with you, wearing proof of your ownership of me." She swallowed. "If you want me."

She'd been right. His eyes were like coals. The way he stared into hers, she had little doubt that he was looking at the same color. When he asked, she'd tell him about the impact the storms were having on her.

"The collar is on the bed," he said. "If you put it on it'll stay there until I say otherwise."

"I understand, Master."

He let go of her hair, placed his hands over her cheeks and guided her mouth to his cock. Whimpering in joy and submission, she parted her lips and slipped them over his length. A blast of wind raked over her spine. Whimpering again, she clamped her legs together. She'd climax when Master said she could.

Her Submission

Excerpt

Chapter One

"You're lucky you weren't killed. I'm sorry, I shouldn't have said that. You're alive and that's what counts."

"Yes, I'm alive."

Five minutes ago, Kaci Winters had nearly gone about her business without talking to the man with the flat tire, but it wasn't as if they didn't know each other. After all, they'd chatted for a whole half-minute earlier in the day. Noticing he'd had trouble kneeling, she'd decided that offering to help was preferable to replenishing the toilet paper in the men's restroom at Pause Awhile Campground. She'd reminded him of their connection, then had taken the lug wrench from him. Once the nuts had become loose, she'd positioned the jack under the car in preparation for lifting it, but he'd taken over.

She hadn't come out and asked what his mobility problem

was, but she had stared. That had probably been why he'd mentioned he'd been in a motorcycle accident. She'd expressed sympathy, but he'd shrugged. She should have dropped what had been none of her business but she'd asked the thirty-something stranger with big hands, broad shoulders, and intense gray eyes about his accident.

"It happened three months ago." He paused while returning her gaze. "Have you ever ridden a motorcycle?"

"A few times, but only as a passenger."

"Boyfriend or husband driving?"

She wasn't surprised by the stranger's attempt to learn something of a personal nature, other than that her favorite ice cream was mint chocolate chip. It came with the territory if you were a decent-looking twenty-three-year-old female and the man asking the question was traveling alone. He wasn't wearing a wedding ring, not that that said anything these days.

Like earlier, his gaze was intense. A little disconcerting. A little exciting.

"The guy and I hadn't known each other that long, so he was kind of a boyfriend," she explained. "The way he handled his bike scared me."

He didn't as much as blink. "Enough so that he became an ex?"

"Pretty much."

She'd gotten to her feet after dealing with the jack but had stayed in close proximity in case the man needed help getting the flat off. Whatever his injuries had been, he hadn't lost upper body strength, as witnessed by the easy way he removed the tire. He'd already gotten out the spare and wasted no time sliding it in place. She liked how he handled himself. There was a smoothness to him, a confidence that made her think he'd emotionally gotten over the accident.

That was something they could talk about — putting the past behind them.

Or she would if she'd been more successful at it.

Earlier in the day, she'd walked up the road a quarter

mile to the café and adjacent ice cream parlor that did great business in the summer as vacationers headed into the mountains. She'd made her purchase and had been sitting at a picnic table when a new pickup with a fancy canopy had pulled into the gravel parking area. A man had gotten out, and headed right for where she'd been sitting, leaned against her table, and stretched. He'd obviously been in no hurry. She'd been a little concerned about personal space, but she often was.

After her initial discomfort, she'd felt herself being drawn to him. There was something intriguing about him, a commanding presence. A deepness to his gaze, as if he was looking for something in her.

For a moment, she'd thought he'd found it, but that was crazy. They were strangers.

He'd asked how much the ice cream cost and whether it was good, which had helped her get past her, what, nervous energy? They'd even engaged in a friendly argument about the best flavors. He'd gone into the parlor and had come out with a double strawberry cone.

"Just what the doctor ordered," he'd told her before slowly getting back into his truck.

All the way back to where she was spending the summer, she'd mulled over the brief connection. He didn't turn her on, but there was something about him she couldn't quite shake, a mysterious aura. A man like that might have a place in her fantasies.

Fortunately, he'd never know what direction her fantasies took.

She'd been surprised and a little suspicious to have him show up at the Pause Awhile Campground where she worked, but his explanation that he'd decided he needed a break from driving and had been taking in the waterfalls off the road between the café and the campground made sense. He'd spotted the Pause Awhile sign just as the driver's side rear tire began to go flat. He'd had no choice but to stop driving so he could deal with it. He certainly hadn't expected to see her.

The longer she watched the man, who hadn't bothered to introduce himself, the more intrigued she became. If his vehicle was any indication, he was better off financially than those who rented RV spaces here. He was traveling by himself and, if she said and did the right things, he might decide to spend the night.

Unless she decided she'd rather sleep alone — which she didn't always want to, because at night her imagination sometimes took her into places she didn't understand. What she labeled sexual fantasies got her hot and bothered, all right. They also left her feeling out of control and confused. Where the hell did they come from?

"The not quite a boyfriend with the motorcycle had some good qualities," she said, by way of continuing the conversation and putting distance between herself and thoughts she didn't need. "A decent job, for one."

"But?"

"But he was into macho, if you know what I mean."

The stranger held out his hand, prompting her to drop a lug nut into his palm. Their fingers didn't touch but came close enough that she'd acknowledged the potential.

"He wanted you to play the little woman?"

"We didn't live together." *I've only done that once. Never again. Maybe.* "He thought that whatever he was doing or wanted to do took priority. I should kick my agenda aside to accommodate him."

"And you're a liberated woman."

Truth was she wasn't certain what label to put on herself. Messed up, for sure. Thinking she was running out of time in which to decide whether she was interested in more than a casual conversation, she watched as he slipped the rest of the lug nuts in place. After lowering the truck, he picked up the lug wrench in preparation for tightening them even more.

"Let me." She held out her hand. "Whoever does this part needs to kneel, and right now that isn't your strong suit."

He stared at her without speaking for so long that she became acutely aware of the male-female component. He wasn't just looking her over, he was going beneath the surface, searching for something he had no intention of sharing with her. It could have been as simple as an older man trying to decide whether a young thing was interested in him, but she didn't think so. She might have been more concerned if they weren't in a public area.

At length, it occurred to her that he was waiting for her to make good on her offer. She took the tool from him and knelt again. It was pushing ninety this afternoon, which was why she had on shorts. Fortunately, he'd pulled onto the grass-weeds that flanked the campground entrance instead of going clear to the rocky area near the office. Her task took a fair amount of upper body strength, but not her full attention. As a result, she remained aware of his presence. He hadn't invaded her personal space the way he had at the ice cream parlor, but neither did she feel apart from him. He struck her as someone accustomed to being in close proximity with another human being. Maybe a wife? Maybe a sex slave?

Sex slave! Where had the thought come from? Damn it, much more of that nonsense and she'd have to see a shrink, something she vowed she'd never do. She wasn't the most squared away person in the world but she was able to function. What more did she want?

A different past.

Done with her task, she looked over her shoulder at the slightly over-six-foot-tall man. His features were in shadow, which made seeing his expression difficult. Being on her knees like this was more intimidating than she wanted to admit. Disconcerting.

And he knew it.

"It's a good thing I don't charge mechanics' rates," she said as she got to her feet. She tightened her hold on the lug wrench. Forget a one-night stand. He was too — something.

"I appreciate it. So" — he looked around — "are you staying

with family or friends?"

"I work here."

"You do?"

She could tell he hadn't expected that, but then most people didn't. "It's a summer job, May through October. I get a place to stay and a not bad salary. Get to meet a lot of different people and occasionally work on my auto repair skills."

His disbelieving expression faded a little, to be replaced by something she didn't understand, but maybe should try to.

"You keep saying 'I'. So it's just you doing, what, being a campground host?"

"It's kind of communal living, only with a constantly changing cast of characters," she said to let him know she wasn't here alone. "I answered a Craigslist ad. They hired me."

"Hmm. It doesn't look like a first-class operation."

"It isn't. People are only supposed to stay for ten days, but my guess is nearly half of the RVs here belong to people who have nowhere else to live. As long as they pay their rent, the owners don't mind."

His nod made her wonder if he could relate, but he didn't strike her as someone who carried his house on his back. His truck was top of the line, his clothes expensive. His dark hair was on the long side. Her guess was he'd been more interested in getting back on his feet after his accident than haircuts.

"All done," she said, indicating the spare tire. "Now you're free to go."

"Free? Yeah, I am."

Unexpectedly, she couldn't think of anything to say. Shouldn't he want to get back on the road? To her way of thinking, she hadn't given out any signals that she was into a roll in the hay. Maybe she'd entertained the thought at first but no longer.

"So you have limitations on how many hours you should

drive in a day?" All right, so it wasn't the most brilliant question she'd ever asked, but hopefully he'd get the hint that it was time for him to move on.

He smiled, one of those grins that didn't reach his eyes and made her think he was doing what he figured was expected. "This is the longest trip I've taken since the accident. Part of it was because I needed a change of scenery."

'Change of scenery.' She could relate to that. Restless. Dissatisfied. Always looking for something.

"Put your feet up the moment you get home and keep going with your physical therapy." What was her problem? One moment she wanted him gone, the next she wanted to learn more about him.

"I'd like to pay you for —"

"No. Helping you allowed me to get my good deed over with for the day."

On the tail of another semi-smile, he held out his hand. "Thanks for the help. Your parents raised an independent woman."

Her so-called parents had had nothing to do with how she'd turned out. She might have dropped that on him if not for the way he held her hand. He didn't have it in a death grip, but she'd have to work at getting loose.

Memories of handcuffs and locked doors stirred. Damn it! Would she never get that nightmare time out of her system? Barely holding onto self-control, she pulled back. He held on a second longer then released her.

"It's been interesting," he said. "One more question and then I'll let you go back to work. What are your plans once summer's over? This place closes down, doesn't it?"

"Yes." What did he mean by 'interesting' and what had the overly long handshake been about?

"Maybe you're in college?"

"I've taken a few courses." The way he studied her made the hairs on the back of her neck stand up. The damn man intimidated and intrigued her at the same time. "I'm not worried about paying the bills. Something always comes up."

The corner of his mouth twitched. "What's that saying, something about a rolling stone not gathering any moss? You aren't interested in settling down?"

What do you care? "No. There's nothing wrong with that."

"I didn't say there was, but most young women have a life plan. Specific goals."

How do I begin to do that? "Sounds boring."

He appeared to be mulling over what she'd just said, searching for flaws in her so-called logic. Well, damn it, what she did or didn't do with her life was none of his business. Going it alone was the only thing she knew.

He opened the cab door. "I hope you find what you're looking for."

"What makes you think that's what I'm doing?"

"Because you are."

More books from
Totally Bound Publishing

Book one in the Carnal Secrets series

Freedom is everything to jockey Marina until an emotionally scarred man kidnaps her. His goal – to dominate his captive in all ways.

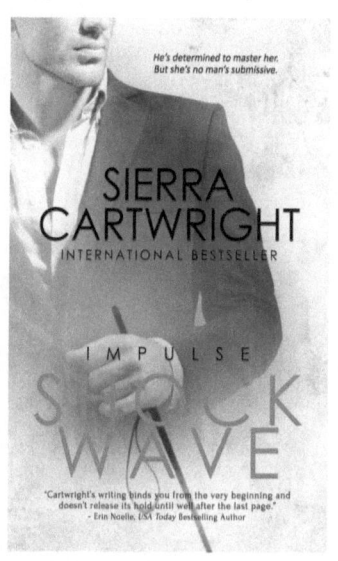

He's determined to master her.
But she's no man's submissive.

SIERRA
CARTWRIGHT
INTERNATIONAL BESTSELLER

IMPULSE

SHOCK
WAVE

"Cartwright's writing binds you from the very beginning and
doesn't release its hold until well after the last page."
- Erin Noelle, USA Today Bestselling Author

Book one in the Impulse series

There can only be one victor…

No one would understand that my submission empowered me, that I felt stronger kneeling at Gabriel's feet than I ever had standing at Paul's side.

Book one in the Bound For Justice series

Targeted by a drug cartel, Teague is out for vengeance until Chantel lands in his lap. Is this fiery, redheaded submissive his lifeline or his downfall?

About the Author

Vonna Harper

What prompts a mild-mannered mostly law abiding woman to write erotica and erotic romance, a lot revolving around BDSM and capture/bondage? Is it the complex issue of taking or giving up control?

Vonna Harper doesn't know and she has given up trying to find the answer. It's enough that many readers are drawn to what some call the dark side. All she asks is that readers understand she writes fiction--a brand of fiction she finds fascinating.

Vonna has lost count of the number of books, novellas, and short stories she's written. What she has no doubt of, it's a hell of a ride.

Vonna Harper loves to hear from readers. You can find contact information, website details and an author profile page at https://www.totallybound.com/

Home of Erotic Romance

www.ingramcontent.com/pod-product-compliance
Lightning Source LLC
Chambersburg PA
CBHW020431180626
46812CB00003B/1174